Wanted . . . Mud Blossom

Wanted . . . Mud Blossom

BETSY BYARS

Illustrated by Jacqueline Rogers

Delacorte Press

054733

Published by
Delacorte Press
Bantam Doubleday Dell Publishing Group, Inc.
666 Fifth Avenue
New York, New York 10103

Library of Congress Cataloging in Publication Data

Byars, Betsy Cromer.
    Wanted . . . Mud Blossom / by Betsy Byars ; illustrated by Jacqueline
Rogers.
        p.   cm.
    Summary: Convinced that Mud is responsible for the disappearance of the
school hamster that he was taking care of for the weekend, Junior Blossom is
determined that the dog should be tried for his "crime."
    ISBN 0-385-30428-5
    [1. Family life—Fiction. 2. Dogs—Fiction.] I. Rogers, Jacqueline, ill. II.
Title.
PZ7.B9836Wan   1991
[Fic]—dc20   90-19881   CIP   AC

Manufactured in the United States of America

September 1991

10 9 8 7 6 5 4 3 2 1

BVG

*For Skippy, Mac, Cookie, Shine,
Lucy, Barney, Kate, Gus, Sport,
Chester, and Harvey*

Contents

Wanted . . . Mud Blossom

Chapter One

Junior's Surprise

"JUNIOR."

Junior was digging under the pine trees. His mother called again from the porch.

"Junior!"

Junior still didn't hear her. He was intent. He dug carefully, lifting shallow scoops of earth on his shovel, then throwing them sideways into the brush. Sweat rolled down his shiny face.

"Junior Blossom!"

Now he looked up. He made a visor with one hand and shaded his eyes from the late afternoon sun.

"What are you up to, Junior?"

"I'm making something."

"Junior . . ."

"It's something for school."

"It doesn't look like something for school. It looks to me like you're digging a hole." This was an accusation.

"No, no, it's not a hole."

Junior looked down at his feet. He had been digging since he got home from school, and as he dug, he covered his excavation carefully with boards. The boards jagged across the pine needles like a streak of wooden lightning.

"A hole is round, Mom. Does this look round?"

He spread out his arms to take in the panorama of his digging.

"Junior Blossom, you know what I told you about holes."

"Yes, I do."

"What?"

"You told me not to dig them. You said people could break their necks falling into holes. You said you knew a cow one time that fell in a hole and you said your daddy made you and your brothers dig a ramp to get it out. You said even though you had not helped your brothers dig the hole, you had to help dig the ramp, which was not fair. See, I remember every single thing you ever told me about holes."

"Then why are you digging one?"

"THIS is NOT a HOLE!" Junior emphasized the important words to get the message across.

"So?" his mom said. "What is it?"

"It's a surprise."

"Junior—"

"A good surprise," he said to ward off what he knew was coming. It came anyway.

"I have had it with your surprises. You made wings that broke both your legs. You made a coyote trap that trapped YOU. And your UFO ended up on Old Man Benson's chicken house."

"This is different, Mom, really. You'll like this one." He

2

stepped over his streak of lightning so he could have a talk with his mother.

He cupped his hands around his mouth to make the talk more intimate. "Mom, remember what I told you last week about school?"

She sighed.

"I said I didn't like it, remember?"

"That was not exactly headline news, Junior. I've heard that before a time or two."

"Well, I take that back. I do like school. I love school. School is my favorite thing in the whole entire world."

"What changed your mind?"

"You'll see on Friday. That's just one more day to wait. This is Thursday. Tomorrow's Friday. Something wonderful is going to happen to me on Friday."

Junior had rested his shovel against his skinny chest, and now he folded his hands over it prayerfully. "Please don't make me tell, Mom. Please! I want it to be a surprise. Please, please, please wait till Friday."

"Junior, don't get down on your knees. If you promise me it's not a hole . . ."

"I promise."

"But if I find out it is a hole . . ."

"You won't. You couldn't. Because it isn't. It's a—" Junior clamped one hand over his mouth.

He had almost told. He had almost blurted out the secret. That was the trouble with a really good secret. It was always trying to slip out on its own.

His mother seemed unaware of how close she had come to hearing the big news. She said, "I don't want any trouble on Friday, Junior; that's when Roon's coming."

"I know that."

3

"I want Roon to think we are a normal, everyday family."

"We are."

"I don't want one single thing to go wrong."

"It won't."

They watched each other across the empty yard for a moment. There was a long silence.

Then Vicki Blossom said, "Well, supper's on the stove—hot dogs." She crossed the yard to the truck. Her steps quickened as she got closer.

"Oh, Junior," she said, more to herself than to her son, "I'm going to the mall and get the best-looking outfit they've got. I want to look beautiful tomorrow!"

"You will."

"So, eat when you get hungry."

"I'm probably too excited to eat." He glanced down. "You know . . . the surprise."

"Well, it's there if you want it. Don't anybody wait up for me. I'm going to be late."

She opened the door to the truck, climbed in, started the engine, and roared out of the yard, leaving a trail of dust behind.

Vern came out on the porch and sat on the top step.

Junior leaned on his shovel. "Don't ask me what I'm making because—"

"I won't ask what you're making because I don't want to know," Vern interrupted.

"But ask me tomorrow and I will tell."

"I'm not going to ask tomorrow or any other day. I wouldn't ask if you begged me. I—"

The phone rang inside the house and Vern got quickly to his feet. "If it's for me," Junior called after Vern, al-

4

though Junior had never gotten a call in his life, "if it's for me, say I'm busy making a surprise."

Vern disappeared into the house, and Junior took his shovel and dug three more scoops of earth. He measured the length of the excavation with his eyes.

It was perfect.

Junior put the last board into place and stepped back. For the first time he saw the completed project.

It took his breath away.

This was the best thing he had ever made in his life. Junior put his hand over his heart to keep it from bursting out of his chest with pride.

He closed his eyes for a moment, as if he had been looking at something too bright for human eyes to endure. He tried to swallow the lump of emotion in his throat. Then he opened his eyes and looked again at his invention.

This time Junior tried to look at his invention critically, as if he were Vern. He tried to find fault with it. But he couldn't. There was no fault. Perfection, absolute perfection, lay at his feet.

When Junior was small, he used to say things like, "Good-bye, house" and "good-bye, red hill." But the family was always saying, "Junior, stop that. Hills and houses can't hear you."

"Maybe . . . maybe not," Junior would answer.

But now there was no one to hear him, to make fun of him.

"Hello, tunnel," Junior said softly.

He picked up the shovel, and walking backwards so he could admire his work as long as possible, like a procession in reverse, Junior moved toward the house.

Vern picked up the phone. "Hello?"

"Vern, is that you?" It was his best friend Michael.

"Yes."

"Vern, has anything happened?"

Michael's voice was a whisper. Even though Vern was alone in the house, he lowered his voice too.

"No, we're still all right."

"She hasn't told on us?"

"No."

"Do you think she will?"

"Well, it's been . . ." Vern paused to count the days on his fingers. It had happened Saturday, so there were Sunday, Monday, Tuesday, Wednesday, and today was Thursday. Almost five whole days. "It's been five days," he whispered.

"Do you think if she was going to tell, she already would have?"

"I hope so."

"I'm still scared, are you?"

"I'm still scared."

"Mad Mary is the scariest woman in the world."

Vern could not disagree with that. "Yes."

"But how are we going to get our backpacks?"

"I haven't figured that out."

"Mine's Boy Scout, and it's got my name on it. My mom's already asked me where it is."

"What did you say?"

"I said I left it at your house. We have to go back to get it; but if we do, I'm afraid she'll kill us."

"I'm afraid she'll kill us too. She wanted to kill us last time."

Junior spoke from the doorway. "Who wanted to kill you? What are you talking about?"

6

Vern said quickly, "I got to go. Big Ears just walked in."
He hung up the phone.

"Who wanted to kill you?" Junior persisted.

"Nobody."

"I'll tell you about my surprise if you'll tell me who
wanted to kill you."

"Nobody! How many times do I have to tell you? Nobody!"

Vern ran up the steps into his room and slammed the
door behind him.

Chapter Two

Mystery by the Roadside

"I KNOW YOU'RE TIRED OF HEARING ABOUT MY SUMMER, Ralphie, but I can't stop talking about it."

"I noticed that."

"I mean, I was disappointed at first that Pap and Vern and Junior didn't go on the rodeo circuit with Mom and me; but really, Ralphie, the truth is that Vern and Junior are still children and Mom and I are . . ." She paused.

"Women." Ralphie said the word in a flat voice that made it unflattering.

"And there's always next summer. We can all go then."

"I thought the family was going to settle down—stay home."

Maggie was on the back of Ralphie's bicycle. Ralphie was pedaling. They were moving slowly up the hill toward the Blossom farm.

"Well, we are . . . eventually—" She broke off. "Oh, stop, Ralphie, there's a turtle."

8

"The turtle's making better time than I am."

"Please, Ralphie."

Ralphie moved to the side of the road and stopped. "Maggie, this is a hill, and when we stop on a hill, it's hard to get started."

"I'll walk the rest of the way. Every time I see a turtle on the road, I just have to stop and help it across, don't you?"

"Not really." Ralphie shook his head. Sweat flew.

"October's the turtle-mating season, did you know that?"

"No, but this is the third turtle you've made me stop for. These turtles need to cool down."

"I think it's romantic the way they cross highways and ditches for the turtles they love."

Ralphie thought it was romantic the way he was pedaling up an impossible hill for the girl he loved, but he said nothing.

"I would just hate it if while this turtle was rushing toward her lover, a truck came by."

Maggie picked up the turtle. It drew back into its shell, but the legs continued to walk in the air.

Maggie looked at the turtle's face as she carried it across the road.

"Ralphie, do you think she's on her way to one particular turtle?"

"I wouldn't know."

There was the sound of a car horn and Maggie glanced over her shoulder. She said, "Oh, it's my mom. Mom!" She waved with her free hand.

Vicki Blossom honked again. "Supper's on the stove!" she called as she passed them. Then she gunned the mo-

tor, and the truck disappeared over the top of the next hill.

"My mom has a new boyfriend, did I tell you?"

"I thought she liked the bull rider."

"No, that's over."

"So what does this guy do?"

"Ralphie, my mom has fallen in love with a horse detective. My mom could not fall in love with someone who sells hardware or drives a bus. She has to fall in love with a horse detective."

"Well, I guess somebody's got to."

"It's like, well, somebody buys a horse and insures it for a hundred thousand dollars. This happens, Ralphie. Then the horse dies. So then this man—his name is Rooney— gets hired by the insurance company to prove it was murder. Which he usually does."

"You like him?"

"I haven't met him yet, but my mom has told me a lot about how people kill horses and it would make even you sick, Ralphie."

"Why do you say 'even you'? I'm human, Maggie, hard as it may be for you to believe."

"Ralphie, they hook them up to electricity. They suffocate them; one time somebody put Ping-Pong balls up a horse's nose."

"Yes, that makes even me sick."

"This weekend he's coming out to the farm, and we have our orders. We are to pretend we are a normal, everyday family, which we aren't!"

"I agree."

"Maybe we can pretend to be normal for an hour or two, but not for a whole weekend. We Blossoms have never been just anybody."

11

"No."

Ralphie glanced down. There was a flower at Maggie's feet, and Ralphie bent to pick it. He stood with it in his hand, as if deciding what to do with it. Then he leaned forward and worked the stem into Maggie's braid.

Maggie smiled. "That was nice, Ralphie."

"I'm always nice."

"You know what I want to do when we get home?" Maggie jumped the ditch and set the turtle on the ground, facing the woods. "Off you go!" she said encouragingly.

What Ralphie wanted to do was collapse on the front porch in a rocking chair. His legs hurt.

Ralphie had an artificial leg—the result of an accident with a power mower three years earlier. He now had the best artificial leg made—a Cat-Cam—but even a real leg couldn't take the strain of pedaling Maggie up and down hills all day.

"I thought we were going to eat supper. Your mom said . . ."

"Well, we are; but after that I'd like to get Sandy Boy and go—"

She broke off. "Ralphie! Look!"

"Maggie, if it is another romantic turtle—"

"No! Ralphie! Look!" She pointed to the weeds at her feet.

There was an urgency in Maggie's voice that made him forget his discomfort. He moved toward the ditch.

Ralphie shielded his eyes. "What am I supposed to be looking at?"

"There."

Maggie bent and reached into the tall grass. She pulled up a stained cloth bag. "Don't you know what this is?"

"Here's my first guess—a stinking bag."

12

"Ralphie, this is Mad Mary's bag." Her voice was low with concern. "This is the bag she carries with her all the time. Ralphie, she collects things to eat in this bag."

"So?"

"So she would never be without this if . . . if she could help it. . . ."

There was a silence. A truck rounded the curve, sounding its horn, and Ralphie moved his bicycle onto the shoulder of the road.

Maggie glanced in annoyance at the truck for interrupting.

"This bag was part of Mad Mary, just like her cane. You remember her cane, don't you?"

Ralphie nodded. He did remember that cane. Mad Mary had loaned it to him and Maggie the night they climbed the tree together. "That was the cane," he said, "that she loaned us the night—"

"Yes."

"Let me finish. The night we climbed up in the tree and you kissed me."

"I did not kiss you."

"Well, you kissed me back. It's the same thing. You can't deny you kissed me back, Maggie."

"Ralphie, I'm serious."

"I am too. Girls kissing me back is very serious to me."

"Ralphie, this bag was part of Mad Mary. She would never just abandon this bag . . ." She opened the handles and looked inside.

"Oh, Ralphie."

Ralphie sighed. "What now?"

"Ralphie, it's a dead possum. Now I know something's happened to her."

"How?"

"She would never abandon a dead possum. This is her supper. She makes varmint stew out of them. Junior's eaten it."

Ralphie ran one hand through his red hair. He let both hands come to rest on his hips.

"Ralphie, something terrible has happened to Mad Mary."

Ralphie was silent. Concern for turtles, for Mad Mary. Even dead possums got more concern than he did.

"Ralphie, we've got to get home fast."

With a sigh, Ralphie pushed his bicycle onto the road.

Maggie jumped the ditch and sat on the seat of the bicycle. She clutched his thin shoulders.

Ralphie put his weight on the pedal and they started slowly up the hill.

"Does this mean," he asked hopefully, "that we won't be stopping for turtles?"

Chapter Three

The Secret Secret

"I KNOW THE BEST SECRET ABOUT MYSELF IN THE world," Junior said.

"That's good," Pap answered.

Junior and Pap were on the front porch. Pap was in the rocking chair. Junior stood balancing on the railing, eating a hot dog wrapped in a slice of white bread. Mustard oozed out the end.

Junior's dirty toes curled over the edge of the railing for support. Between bites, his arms waved gently up and down for balance.

"And you'd wish I'd tell you the secret, right?" Junior asked.

"Well . . ."

"You'd give anything to know, right?"

"Well, not anything."

Junior stuffed the last of his hot dog in his mouth, and he

lost his balance. He swung his arms around, windmill-like, until he was steady again.

He swallowed his hot dog and went on about his secret. When Junior had a secret, he felt more alive, more special, than at any other time.

"There are two reasons why I can't tell you. One, I'm not supposed to tell you anything that would excite you, Mom says, and—"

"Junior, I had one little heart attack."

"Not a little one, Pap. Remember, I saw it."

"Well, a heart attack. I think I can take the strain of hearing your secret."

"You didn't let me finish," Junior said. "Two, if I told you, it wouldn't be a secret anymore."

Pap shook his head back and forth. "Junior, Junior, Junior," he said.

Junior lost his balance for good and jumped down onto the porch. Then he sat and crossed his legs.

"Why did you say, 'Junior, Junior, Junior'?"

"It just came out."

"I don't like people to say my name but one time— Junior, like that. It was all right for people to say three Juniors in a row when I was little, but now I just want one at a time."

"I'll remember."

Junior pulled a thread on his shorts. The thread kept coming, getting longer and longer. Junior kept pulling. Then he saw that he had pulled out the hem. He folded the hem back under and patted it in place.

"Actually, my secret came just at the right time. I was getting worried about myself."

"Oh? Why is that?"

"See, my other ideas—my wings, my coyote trap, my

UFO—my other ideas just popped into my head, Pap, like magic. Only nothing was popping in my head at all. I thought it had something to do with school."

"Oh."

"Like, we have to use our minds. We have to! Mrs. Wilson makes us! If we forget to use them, she points to her head like that." Junior tapped his temple. "Anyway I was using my mind so much in school that when I got home from school, it just wanted to rest."

"A mind needs to rest every now and then."

"Yes, rest, but maybe resting was the wrong word. My mind wasn't so much resting. It was more like it had gone on strike."

"Right now," Pap said, "I hope I don't get an idea. I hope I'll sit here till the moon comes up without one single idea coming into my head."

"I was so desperate I was ready to start standing on my head like Ralphie."

"Ralphie stands on his head?"

"He says it makes the blood run to his brain and nourish it. He says that's why his brain is so brilliant."

"Well, it's too late for me to be standing on my head. My brain's got to get along with whatever the body chooses to send it. I— Oh, here comes Mud. Mud, you ready for our evening walk?"

Mud was Pap's dog, a big golden dog with a red bandana around his neck. Mud had just come back from one walk, but he was ready for another. He waited at the porch steps, wagging his tail, his eyes bright with anticipation. Mud had never turned down a walk in his life.

Pap got slowly to his feet.

"Pap, you didn't let me finish about my brain."

17

"Well, come on. You can tell me about your brain while we walk."

"Can my dog come too?"

"If he behaves himself."

"He will! Dumpie!" Junior called.

Dump crawled out from under the porch. "We're going for a walk," Junior told him.

Mud was almost to the pine trees, and Dump ran to join him. Then, as if he thought better of it, he stopped.

"I wish Mud and Dump could be friends," Junior said. "Dump's willing."

Mud paused and looked back to see if they were coming.

"We're not going that way," Junior called.

"Mud smells something."

"Well, just because he smells something, that doesn't mean we have to go in that direction."

"You heard Junior," Pap called. "We ain't going that way, Mud."

Mud did not move. He was used to taking the lead. He barked once.

"You go your way, Mud. We'll go ours."

Mud gave them a moment to change their minds. Then he bounded away into the trees.

"That's better. You shouldn't give in to him all the time," Junior said. "Mud's getting spoiled. Ever since we carried him into the hospital to visit you, he's been like that. I caught him trying to eat off the table yesterday."

"He's my pal."

Junior stopped in sudden alarm. "Oh, let's don't go through the pine trees, Pap; please, you'll see the secret. You'll see the surprise!"

"That's the surprise over there—them boards on the ground?"

"Pap, you looked! Now it's ruined. The secret's ruined!"

"Now, now, I didn't see nothing but some boards lying on the ground," Pap protested.

"That's it!"

"But I don't know what you call it," Pap said.

"You don't?"

"No."

"You didn't recognize it?"

"No."

Junior put one dirty hand over his heart. "Ah," he said, "what a relief. My secret is still a secret."

Pap sneaked one final look at the boards lying on the ground under the pine trees. "Junior, Junior—" he broke off. "Sorry—Junior."

Pap glanced back at the house. "You think Vern wants to go with us?"

"No."

"Why not?"

"Because he thinks someone wants to kill him."

"Now, Junior."

"I heard him say that on the phone. He was talking to Michael. I memorized his words. 'I'm afraid she'll kill us too. She wanted to kill us last time.'"

"He and Michael were just up to some foolishness. Nobody wants to kill Vern."

"It didn't sound like foolishness," Junior said. "It sounded like he was really scared."

"That's playacting, but I'll talk to him about it."

Junior squinted up at Pap. "You know something, Pap. I never have to playact. You know why?"

"Why is that?"

19

"Because my real life is so exciting and so full of adventure that I don't have to playact. I just have to live my life!"

"I'm too old to playact. I just live my life too."

"And tomorrow is going to be one of the most exciting days I have ever had in my life. Tomorrow is Friday, isn't it?"

"All day."

"Then tomorrow is when the excitement begins." Junior grinned. He had no idea how true his words would turn out to be.

Chapter Four

Mad Mary Is Missing

"FASTER!"

"I—am—not—a—horse."

Ralphie reminded Maggie of this in what he thought was an extremely nice voice, considering how tired he was of pedaling. Both Ralphie's legs hurt now.

"I know that."

"Well, gimme a break."

Ralphie glanced up at the top of the hill. Sweat rolled down his face, dropped off his chin. Every now and then he had to go sideways to keep from stopping altogether—like right now. He turned toward the center of the road.

"Look, if you're going to waste time weaving from side to side like this," Maggie said, "stop and I'll pedal for a while."

This insult gave Ralphie a sudden burst of anger and new strength. He gained enough speed to proceed up the hill. It would take, Ralphie figured, at least three more bursts of anger to get them to the top.

Keep it up, Maggie, Ralphie thought. Three more insults and we're home.

Ever since Maggie had jumped the ditch and seen Mad Mary's bag, she had been like a woman driven, a woman who— Suddenly Ralphie made the connection.

"You remind me . . ." he said, pausing to draw in a badly needed breath, "you remind me of my mother."

"What?"

"You heard me."

"And just how do I remind you of your mother?" Maggie asked coldly. Ralphie's first words to her this afternoon had been, "I had to get out of the house. The ogress is on the rampage."

Ralphie remembered that unfortunate statement at the same time that Maggie did. He closed his mouth.

"You think I'm an ogress?"

Again, Ralphie did the smart thing and kept his mouth shut.

"I'm waiting to hear if you think I'm an ogress. . . . Oh, Ralphie, hurry up. We're never going to get home at this rate."

Ralphie cleared his throat. "No, you're more like an— oh, I don't know—an ogrette."

"Ogrette!"

"That's a small ogress," Ralphie went on conversationally, "like a dinette or a kitchenette."

"Stop this bicycle!"

"Gladly."

"This minute!"

"It's stopped."

Actually the strength that his anger at Maggie had

given him had worn off, and the bicycle had pretty much stopped on its own.

Ralphie braced his foot on the road. He waited while Maggie climbed off the bicycle.

"Ralphie, I want to say just one thing to you. This is Mad Mary's bag, the bag she collects her food in, and inside the bag"—she pulled the handles apart—"is a possum that has—"

"Seen better days," Ralphie interrupted.

"Don't try to be funny."

"Close the bag, please. One look at a dead possum is enough, Maggie. I don't need to see it twice. And I sure don't need to smell it twice. Throw that thing away."

"Absolutely not."

"Why?"

"It's evidence."

"Of what?"

"Mad Mary may have been kidnapped, and you're wasting time asking stupid questions and calling me names."

"Maggie, people don't go around kidnapping a woman who hasn't had a bath in fifteen years. Now, throw that bag away and get back on the bike."

"If I get back on the bike, this possum gets on with me."

Ralphie breathed in and out twice without speaking.

"And also," Maggie went on, "you'll have to take back what you said—about me being an ogrette."

"I stick by that."

Maggie's green eyes narrowed. "Then I'm not getting on the bike."

"That's up to you."

There was a silence. Ralphie was the one who broke it.

"All day long," he said, apparently speaking to the handlebars of his bicycle, "no, make that all month long,

23

you've been taking me for granted. Do this, Ralphie. Do that. Stop here. Start there . . ."

There was another silence. Ralphie looked up, this time directly at Maggie, who waited for the rest with her arms folded over the dead possum bag.

The flower was still in the end of her pigtail where he had placed it in happier, pre-ogrette times, but it was beginning to wilt.

Ralphie said, "You use me."

Maggie drew in a sharp breath. This was the first time Ralphie had ever said anything critical to her.

Ralphie could see that she was hurt. Well, he said to himself, she wasn't Princess Di. She had to learn how to treat people. Just because she was the most beautiful girl in the world didn't exempt her from being nice. She should be grateful to him for the lesson instead of looking at him like somebody from the North Pole.

Mud burst out of the woods beside them. His nose was in the air. His eyes shone. He jumped the ditch in one graceful leap and closed in on the bag in Maggie's hands.

Mud had smelled this bag from the Blossom porch. It was this bag that had drawn him like a leash through the woods, that had separated him willingly from Pap and Junior and Dump.

And this bag was worth all his efforts.

Maggie let out her breath. "Well."

Ralphie said, "Deep subject."

Maggie said, "I don't think that's funny."

Ralphie said, "I didn't mean it to be."

Mud approached the bag slowly. His eyes were bright with interest. The pungent scent caused the hair to rise on the back of his neck. It was Mad Mary's scent. He knew that scent and distrusted it. But mingled with that scent

24

was the smell of death and of things Mud didn't even know of yet. Mud had never been able to resist the smell of mystery.

He moved closer.

Ralphie said, "So, are you getting on or not? Make up your mind."

"Not."

"Maggie—"

"That would be using you."

She flung the word "using" over her shoulder like an insult. She started up the hill on foot.

Mud, nose in air, followed.

After a minute, Ralphie began pedaling slowly after Maggie and Mud. He kept fifty yards between them; this was enough distance so Maggie couldn't hear if he was back there or not. He knew she was too mad to turn around and look.

Maggie made the turn into the farm. She crossed the bridge. She still hadn't looked back.

Ralphie continued to follow. He coasted down the hill and brought his bike to a stop by the Blossoms' front porch.

Maggie was in the house calling, "Pap! Pap!"

Vern's voice answered, "Pap and Junior went for a walk."

"Which way?"

"I don't know. There are hot dogs on the stove, but they taste funny."

"Vern, look."

"At what?"

"Vern, this is Mad Mary's bag—the one she collects food in."

25

"What?" Vern must have jumped up from the table fast, because Ralphie heard his chair tip over.

"We found it beside the road, Vern. Something terrible has happened to Mad Mary."

"What?"

"I think she's been kidnapped."

"Why?"

"It's just what I think. Something's happened to her, or she wouldn't have dropped this bag. And I'm going to find out what!"

Maggie came back on to the porch. Now, for the first time since the argument, she looked at Ralphie.

"Oh, are you still here?" she asked.

"No, Maggie, I'm not here. I went home."

Maggie sat down on the steps. She held Mad Mary's bag on her lap for a moment and then shoved it to the side. She looked down at her pigtail and saw the drooping flower in the end. Ralphie thought she might take this opportunity to pluck it out, throw it to the ground, and grind it to death with the heel of her tennis shoe.

Ralphie held his breath.

Maggie sighed. She lifted her head and looked at the trees.

Mud was the only one in motion, but it was slow motion. Mud didn't want anyone to notice he was closing in on the bag. His nose had started to run.

In a crawl, pulling himself along with his front paws, he reached the bag. He stretched out his head and rested it on the handles. He lay as if he were asleep, but he had never been more awake in his life.

He breathed deeply, trying to puzzle out the various smells. The sounds of his deep inhalations were the only sounds on the porch.

Maggie glanced at Ralphie out of the sides of her eyes. "There are hot dogs on the stove."

"No, thanks," Ralphie said. "I'm not all that hungry anymore." He kept standing there.

Ralphie had fallen in love with Maggie two years ago in a hospital room. She had been sitting on Junior's bed, her green eyes shining. Even if she hadn't been telling the story of how she and Vern had busted into City Jail, he would have fallen in love with her.

He still loved her. He guessed he always would.

He kept standing there. He wanted to go home—he had never wanted anything more in his life—but he couldn't.

This was what love did to a man, he thought unhappily; it affected the feet. It literally nailed a man to the ground.

He looked down at his feet.

Suddenly Maggie yanked the bag out of Mud's reach. "No, Mud, leave that alone! Bad dog!"

She gave Ralphie another sideways look. "If you don't want a hot dog, you might as well go."

"That's what I was thinking."

"Well, go!"

She sounded as if she were talking to Mud instead of a person.

To Ralphie's surprise and relief, his feet came loose from the ground. And as if he were not taking part in a miracle, as if walking like this were a perfectly normal, everyday occurrence, Ralphie slung one leg over his bike.

"Good-bye," she called after him.

Without turning around he said, "Good-bye, Maggie." He was pleased that his good-bye sounded more final than her good-bye.

Legs aching, heart breaking, Ralphie headed for home.

Chapter Five

The Crook in the Grass

"Pap!"

Maggie ran to meet Pap and Junior at the edge of the woods. Her braids flew out behind her.

"Pap, something terrible's happened!"

Pap stopped in place. He put one hand over his heart as if to protect it.

"Your mom?" he said.

"No. No, Pap, it's Mad Mary."

"Mary?"

"Yes, Ralphie and I found her bag by the road—you know, her food bag! The bag was there and she wasn't. I think she's been kidnapped."

Pap's elbows trembled a little as his mind worked over the news. "Mary Cantrell?"

"Yes, Pap, and she's never without that bag."

"No, I don't believe she is."

"I think she had a struggle with someone, and during

28

the struggle she dropped the bag so she could defend herself and . . ."

"Mary's bag."

"Yes, Pap, and there was a possum in it. Pap, when was the last time you saw her alive?"

"Well, let's see. It was last month, I guess. Me and Vern were collecting cans and she gave us a wave."

"I saw her two weeks ago," Junior piped up. "She came by the house. She said, 'Junior, a black snake's taken up residence in a corner of my cave.' She said, 'Come see him, if you'd like.' I said, 'I will.' She said, 'Don't wait too long. He might decide to travel.' I said, 'I won't.' She said—"

Pap interrupted with, "But there didn't seem to be anything wrong?"

"No."

"This is important, Junior. Did she have her bag?"

Junior rolled his eyes up in his head, as if to find the answer there.

"Yes."

"You're sure?"

"Yes, because it was full of nuts and she offered me some."

"I wish we knew somebody who'd seen her after that." Pap started up the steps and his eyes fell on Vern. "You haven't seen her, have you, Vern?"

Vern cleared his throat. "Where would I see her?"

"I was just hoping." He turned to Maggie. "Where exactly did you find this bag?"

"I could show you. It's not far. Why?"

"Because I want to look for the cane. If her cane's there, too, I'll start to worry. Let's go. Vern, you coming?"

"Why would I come?"

"To help!"

Vern came slowly down the steps and trailed after the rest of them.

"But why would anybody want to kidnap her?" Junior asked as they started through the trees.

Maggie said, "Ralphie asked the same question, and I didn't know the answer; but since then I've been thinking about it. Pap, I think Mad Mary's rich. She could be, Pap. Her family was."

"She could be."

"Well, I'm like Pap," Junior said. "I'm not going to start worrying until I see her cane, and I mean it."

"Uh-oh."

The breath went out of Pap as he saw the cane. It lay at his feet in the grass.

"Uh-oh."

The cane had been made long ago from a birch tree and was shaped like a shepherd's crook. Local kids were scared of it. They said, "She'll catch you with it and cook you in a pot."

But Junior loved this cane.

He bent now and picked it up. The cane was taller than he was.

He had admired Mary's way with her cane, the way she could part the forest with it was like something from the Bible. He had fashioned canes for himself, but his canes had not held the magic that hers did.

Now, in his own hands, the magic seemed to have gone out of hers as well.

He reached up and encircled the cane with his fingers. He chose the exact spot where she held the cane, and he knew he was right because the wood had been darkened there with the oil from Mary's hand.

"Now are you starting to worry?" Maggie asked.

Pap nodded.

"Now do you believe me?"

"Yes," Pap said, "I believe."

Vern ran back to the house so he could make a telephone call without being heard. He dialed Michael's number.

Michael's mother answered, and his heart sank. He tried to give his voice an official sound.

"Could I speak to Michael, please? This is an emergency."

"What kind of emergency, Vern?"

"I've got to tell him something that he really, really needs to know."

"You've already talked to him once. You should have told him then."

"I didn't know then."

"Michael," she called, "are you through studying?"

"Yes."

"Then you can talk on the phone for five minutes."

"Michael," Vern said. He was suddenly short of breath. "Guess what?"

"What?"

"Something happened to Mad Mary."

"What?"

"I don't know. They found her bag and cane by the road. Maggie thinks she was kidnapped."

"I don't believe anybody could kidnap her."

"Me either."

"So what do you think?"

"Well, I think maybe she dropped them there on purpose."

Michael drew in his breath. "Yes! She dropped them to make everyone think she had been kidnapped."

"Yes!"

"And you and I would get the word and go back to the cave and she really would kill us this time."

"But if we don't go to the cave—" Vern lowered his voice. "My family's coming in. I can't talk. Junior's already heard too much."

"I can't talk either," Michael whispered.

"Save me a seat on the bus."

"Right."

Vern hung up the phone and was standing innocently by the sink when the family came in the kitchen.

Chapter Six
Mud in the Basement

FRIDAY MORNING CAME AT LAST. NO ONE IN THE BLOS-som family had slept well. Pap was worried about Mary. Maggie was worried about being an ogrette. Vern was worried about being found out. Vicki was worried that her new pants suit was too loud.

Junior couldn't sleep for two reasons. One, he was worried about Mary. He actually wanted to worry about her because she was his best friend in the world. But then in the middle of his worrying, the thought of his surprise would pop up like a bubble of joy, and he wouldn't be able to sleep because he felt bad about feeling so good.

Junior was the first one dressed and he was in the kitchen, fixing a breakfast of peanut-butter toast, when the others came in.

"Is this gorgeous or is this gorgeous?" Vicki Blossom asked. She danced into the kitchen, holding her new pants suit against her.

"Oh, Mom, it's beautiful!" Maggie said.

"You really like it? It's not too . . . loud?" Vicki Blossom walked across the kitchen. She paused at the sink to look at her reflection in the mirror there.

"No, you look good in bright colors."

"I've got a friend who does people's colors, and that's what she said too. It was way too expensive, but . . ." She smiled at herself. "You only live once."

"Once is probably going to be enough for me," Pap told his coffee cup.

"Now, Pap," Vicki Blossom said. "You need to get a new suit."

"It takes more than a suit when you're seventy-five years old."

"I couldn't sleep last night for worrying that it was too loud."

"It's perfect. It's . . ." Maggie searched for the right word. "It's you!"

Mud lay under the sink. He was dividing his attention between two things—Mad Mary's bag, which hung out of reach on a coat hook, and Dump, who was standing in the doorway and looked like he wanted to come into the room.

Mud had control over Dump. Dump was scared of him. And all Mud had to do to stop Dump from coming close was to let out a growl pitched so low that no human ears could hear it.

Dump took two steps into the room. Mud gave his warning growl, and Dump stopped.

Mud turned his eyes back to the bag.

The bag . . . that bag.

Mud had actually gotten possession of the bag last night.

When the family was distracted, he had taken a corner of the bag in his mouth and was halfway out the door before Pap noticed.

"Oh, no, you don't."

Mud had frozen. He'd looked up at Pap, but he hadn't let go. He needed this bag. He needed to take it somewhere private and sort out the smells. Afterwards, he would roll on it to keep the smell with him.

"Drop it, Mud. I said, drop it!"

But Mud couldn't, so Pap twisted it free.

"Mary'll want that back. That bag's important to her. I doubt she's going to want that possum though. It's getting rank."

Pap, with Mud at his heels, had gone outside and tossed the dead possum into the brush. Mud did not leap off the porch to check out the dead possum, because it wasn't the possum that interested him.

Now Mud's look intensified as a breeze came through the open door, carrying the scent to Mud under the sink. The scent called and yet repelled him.

At the table Junior let out a sigh. "I'm trying not to be happy about the surprise, but sometimes I can't help myself. I'm trying as hard as I can but—"

"I'm trying hard to be happy," Vicki Blossom said. "And right now I'm succeeding. Wipe your mouth, Junior, you've got a milk mustache."

Junior blotted his mouth obediently on his arm.

"Well, after breakfast I'm going to have to look for Mary," Pap said. "We're all the family she's got."

"After breakfast I'm going to school. I have to," Junior said. "But no matter what happens, I'm not going to be happy."

Vicki put her hands on her hips. She said, "Pap, surely

you're not going to walk all the way to Mary's cave. That's miles."

"I don't think you ought to go either," Vern said quickly. This was the first time he had spoken. "Mom, don't let him go."

"I got to. Walking's good for me."

"Not that far."

"It is far, Pap," Vern said.

Maggie pushed back her cereal bowl. "You know what Ralphie had the nerve to call me?"

"What?" Junior asked.

"An ogrette."

"What is that, hon?" Vicki Blossom asked. "I never heard of such."

"Maybe he got it out of a fairy story," Junior suggested. "It's probably a compliment."

"It's no compliment. He calls his mom an ogress." Maggie threw her braids behind her back. "He also said I used people, which is not true. I never use people. I'm beginning to think I don't like Ralphie anymore."

Pap shoved back his chair, stood up, adjusted his overall straps, and started for the door. Mud looked up in a questioning way.

Pap didn't call, but Mud came out from under the sink anyway. His ears were up, his tail high.

He moved over to the coat hook and stood under it, looking up at the bag so that Pap would know it was still on his mind.

"Sorry, pal," Pap said.

Pap reached down with one hand and took Mud by his bandana. Mud hated for anybody—even Pap—to do that.

"It's the basement for you."

He began to pull Mud back across the kitchen. Mud, of

36

course, resisted. There was only one thing in the part of the kitchen he was being pulled toward—the basement door.

Mud stiffened his legs, bracing with all his might. As they passed the sink, Mud tried to get back under it, but Pap slid him past the sink, the stove.

At the refrigerator, Mud tried a second tactic—he went limp and fell on his side. Pap continued to slide him easily on the worn linoleum.

"I'm sorry, old pal, but you and Mary don't get along. You can't go with me this time."

Pap opened the basement door. Mud tried a desperate move—a sideways, twisting leap—but Pap was prepared. He turned Mud as if he were twirling a rope, and Mud found himself where he most didn't want to be—on the top step of the basement stairs.

Pap closed the door.

Usually Mud could sense these things. He had a sixth sense when something bad was going to happen to him, and he was always right. It was a kind of dread that came just before baths and scoldings. Even before humans knew they were going to scold him or bathe him, Mud knew.

If he had not been so intent on the bag and keeping Dump out of the kitchen, he would have known about the basement.

Before Pap was out of the kitchen, Mud started to howl. Ahwooo-ooo-oooooo.

"If I didn't know that was a dog, I'd think this was a horror movie," Vicki Blossom said. "Which it practically is."

Junior got up. "I'm going to the bus stop."

"Junior, you've got half an hour."

37

"I'm sorry," Junior said apologetically, "I can't wait."

At the door, he turned.

"And, Pap, if you get to Mary's cave and she's there, and she's all right, tell her I worried about her so much I could hardly enjoy my surprise."

"I'll tell her," Pap said.

Vern got to his feet too. His food was untouched.

"Don't tell me you're eager to go to school too. Will wonders never cease," Vicki Blossom said.

"I'm not so eager to get to school," Vern admitted slowly. He realized he had to be very, very careful what he said from now on. "I'm eager to see Michael. I have some important things to tell him."

Vern and Junior went out of the house together. When they were down the steps, and out of hearing, Vern snapped, "Thanks a lot."

"What? For what?"

"For telling Pap that somebody wanted to kill me."

"Well, if someone wanted to kill me," Junior said reasonably, "I'd want everybody to know about it."

"Well, I don't. And I'll get even with you. You just wait and see."

Chapter Seven
The Cage

Junior sat on the front seat of the school bus. It was three fifteen in the afternoon, and Junior was on his way home.

Junior was jiggling his knees. Junior always jiggled like this when he was excited.

On Junior's lap, jiggling along with Junior, was a wire cage.

"Vern! Vern, look," Junior had said as soon as Vern got on the bus.

"At what?" Vern had looked around as if he didn't know what he was supposed to be looking at. He checked the bus driver, the window, the girls across the aisle, everything but the wire cage on Junior's lap.

"Vern!"

Junior pointed to the cage.

"Oh," Vern said. "Big deal, a mouse."

"No! No, it's a hamster!"

"Same difference."

"No, no, it's—"

"Is that what you've been carrying on about all week—a stupid hamster?" Vern asked with scorn.

Junior nodded. "I get to keep him the whole weekend."

"Well, keep him out of my room."

"Come on, Vern," Michael said. "We got to make plans."

Michael had pulled Vern to the back of the bus, and they sat with their heads together in their usual seat.

To Junior, the cage on his lap was a miracle. He, HE had been selected to take the class hamster home. And he had never been selected for anything in his life. And he was picked first! Before any of the kids in the good reading group. The teacher had picked him first.

And now he was in charge of Scooty for the whole weekend. For the whole weekend, he would look after Scooty, feed Scooty, make things for Scooty.

"And I've already made you a tunnel," Junior said, his lips against the wire of the cage.

The cage smelled of cedar shavings and seeds, and Junior inhaled with pleasure. He loved the smell of a hamster cage. As far as Junior was concerned, the scent could be bottled like perfume for ladies. When he got big, he would sure go for a lady who smelled like a hamster cage.

The bus stopped to let off the Rankin girls. Junior moved the cage slightly into the aisle in case they wanted to admire Scooty as they passed.

"Watch it!" one said, so Junior drew the cage close again.

"Wait till you see the tunnel, Scooty," Junior continued as the bus started up again. "You will love it. It's long and

40

there are little secret rooms at each end and in the secret rooms are—"

The bus stopped again. This time Rebecca from his room got off. "Bye, Junior. Bye, Scooty," she said.

Junior said, "Bye." He wished he could get Scooty out and wave one of his paws at Rebecca, but the bus was already on its way again.

There was always a special festive, free-at-last air about the school bus on Fridays. Junior loved Fridays. He had been looking forward to this one all week and now it was really here. And, during the morning, Junior had figured out that by now Pap would have gotten to the cave and seen that Mary was all right.

Therefore, it was all right for Junior to go ahead and be a little happy. Normally he wouldn't have let himself do this until he heard Pap say, "False alarm. She's right as rain," but this was the most special occasion in Junior's year. Mary would want him to be happy.

"This is your stop, Junior," the bus driver said.

Junior looked up in amazement. "Already?" The only thing wrong with Fridays was that they went so fast.

The driver nodded and opened the door.

Junior got up. "It's a good thing you told me." He put Scooty's cage carefully under one arm. "I was taking care of the hamster and I lost track of everything. Did I tell you I get to keep Scooty all weekend?"

"You told me when you got on."

Junior stood at the foot of the steps with the cage in his arms and waited for Michael and Vern to get off. Then he said, "Look, I got to bring the class hamster home."

"You told me. You told me," Vern said in tired disgust.

"But I didn't tell Michael. Michael, I got to bring the class hamster home."

Michael said, "Neato."

Junior said, "See, Vern, Michael thinks it's neat."

Junior paused. The bus pulled away, leaving the three of them in a cloud of exhaust fumes.

Michael and Vern began to walk to the Blossoms' house, talking in low voices. Junior followed.

"Vern," he said. Vern didn't turn around.

Junior was used to being ignored by Vern, but sometimes Michael was nice to him. One time last week, Vern and Michael had tied him up in a game of outlaw, and Michael had come back and untied him. If it had been up to Vern, Junior thought, he would still be tied up to the tree. Remembering Michael's kindness, Junior directed his words to him.

"Michael, you can see the surprise now if you want to." He added in a rush of forgiveness, "Vern, you can too."

Vern waved him on with a gesture of disinterest.

"Well, I offered," Junior said. He started down the hill backward, giving them a chance to change their minds.

Michael and Vern went into the house, and Junior couldn't wait any longer. With the cage against his chest, he hurried to the pine trees.

He stood for a moment looking at the tunnel he had made the day before. The beauty of it, the range—he couldn't believe he had made it. It made him think of the Great Wall of China. There was a picture of the Great Wall in the library at school, and the librarian had told them it was the only man-made structure that could be seen from outer space. This tunnel had the same panoramic sweep, the same scope as that wall. The Great Tunnel of Junior.

"I made that for you," he told Scooty. "It's the first real tunnel you've ever had. Nobody ever thought to do that for you before."

Junior dropped to his knees as if he were in a sacred place.

"It's got little rooms at each end. I put seeds in one room. That is the dining room. The other room has soft grass. You can sleep in that room. I'll show you both rooms."

Junior lifted one of the boards. "That's the dining room."

He crawled to the other end and lifted the last board. "That's the bedroom. Those are the two main rooms, but there are lots of little cubbyholes, like right there and right there."

Junior paused. He felt like a real estate agent showing off a particularly fine property.

"I don't know whether to put you in the dining room or the bedroom." He looked intently into Scooty's little beadlike eyes. "Are you hungry or sleepy?"

Junior opened the cage, reached in, and took Scooty in his hand. He loved the way Scooty felt, soft and small. It made Junior feel strong and protective.

He remained on his knees with Scooty against his chest. Then he bent forward and put Scooty in the bedroom. He covered him with the board.

"There."

Junior wished he had used see-through boards. It would give him a lot of pleasure to watch Scooty in bed, in his dining room, running through the tunnel, discovering the little cubbyholes.

Maybe he could get some plastic and . . .

No, Junior told himself forcefully, he hadn't made this tunnel for his own pleasure. He had made it for Scooty, and Scooty needed privacy.

Junior stretched out on his stomach and placed his ear

against the board. He could hear nothing, but he still enjoyed lying with his cheek against the warm board.

It was so pleasant, Junior felt he could spend all afternoon like this. He might even bring out a blanket tonight and—

Suddenly Junior lifted his head.

Mary.

He got to his knees.

Pap had to be home by now. Pap would have news. And the news was going to be good. Junior could almost hear Pap's cheerful "False alarm."

Junior got up and ran for the house.

Chapter Eight
Police Call

"FALSE ALARM?" JUNIOR CRIED AS HE ENTERED THE kitchen.

Pap didn't turn around. He was standing by the table, talking to Vern and Michael.

"So what were you doing in her cave?" Pap was asking.

Junior put the hamster cage on the table and took a seat. Vern shot him a look of hatred.

"And I know you both were there because I saw your backpacks."

Vern knew he had to answer, just as Michael would have had to answer if his mother were asking the question.

"Well . . ."

"Spit it out."

"Michael wanted to see Mary's cave. And I said that I'd show it to him. We were just going to look at it from the outside."

Vern swallowed aloud.

"So we got there, and we couldn't see good because it's all overgrown, so we went up on the porch. And I knocked."

"He did knock," Michael said. "He did it with a rock."

"But she didn't answer, so we decided to step inside. And we did. And, gradually, we walked inside a little bit. It was dark and we couldn't see. And we walked in a little bit more. Then we took off our backpacks and we were just standing there—we didn't touch anything! Not one single thing, did we, Michael?"

"No!"

"And then we, we heard s-something behind us . . ."

Vern took a deep breath. As long as he lived he would remember turning around in that dark, dank cave and seeing Mad Mary framed in the entrance.

With the light behind her and the wind blowing her skirts, she looked ten feet tall. Her feet were apart and her hands were braced on either side of the entrance as if to block them from leaving.

"What do you want?" she had asked in a voice made of gravel.

"Nothing, we don't want anything."

"Then what are you doing here?"

"Looking."

She stepped toward them.

Michael put his hands over his eyes.

"Don't you know what I do with kids that trespass in my cave?"

"No."

"I cook them and eat them."

"You're just saying that to scare us."

"And I did scare you, didn't I?"

47

"Yes."

"Enough so you'll leave me alone?"

"Yes."

"Then get going! Shoo!"

She stepped aside and Michael and Vern ran for the outside and life. Not until they were safely at Vern's house, collapsed on the porch, did they realize they'd left their backpacks behind.

"Mr. Blossom," Michael asked, "did you say you saw our backpacks there?"

"Yes."

"What did you do with them?"

"They're right over yonder on the counter."

"Can we have them?"

"You can have them when you give me your word you ain't going to bother Mary again."

"We promise."

"She's got enough problems without you boys harassing her."

"Yes, sir."

"Now, get your backpacks and get out of here. I got to call the police." The boys got up, grabbed the backpacks, and ran for the front door.

"On Mary?" Junior asked.

"Yes."

"I don't think Mary would want you to call the police."

"I got to. I'm about the only person there is that's interested enough."

"You didn't see her?"

"Nope, not a trace."

"I shouldn't have let myself get happy about the surprise," Junior said woefully. "I wouldn't have if I'd known Mary was still missing."

He looked so miserable that Pap pulled him against him and ran one hand through his hair.

"I got time to hear about the surprise, I reckon."

"No, you better go ahead and call the police. I'll get the phone book."

"Go on about the surprise, Junior, while I'm dialing."

"Well, this is it." Junior put one hand on the hamster cage. The exercise wheel spun a little.

Pap glanced at the cage as he reached for the phone book.

"The emergency numbers are on the first page," Junior commented. He began to play with the cage, opening and shutting the door, turning it around on the table, opening the door again.

"Seems like that's the only numbers we ever need around here."

Pap dialed, then hung up in disgust. "Busy. Lord knows how many crimes go unreported because some cop's wife is calling him to bring home a loaf of bread."

In the pause that followed Junior said, "Pap." He moved his fingers back and forth across the wire of the cage, making a musical sound.

"That is the surprise you've been talking about all week —an empty cage?"

Junior was so eager to clear up the misunderstanding that he began sputtering. "No, no, there was something in the cage, but I took it out. See, we have this hamster in our room. His name is Scooty. We voted on the name. Some of the other nominations were Blackie and Fuzzy, but Scooty won. Anyway, every weekend somebody gets to take Scooty home . . ."

Junior attempted to swallow his excitement.

"Slow down, Junior," Pap said.

49

"I can't. I'm trying to. So this weekend was my weekend. That's what I was doing all day yesterday—I was making a tunnel for Scooty. See, Scooty never gets to have any fun—he spends all his time in a cage, going round and round—so I thought this weekend I'd give Scooty the best time of his life. It would be like going to vacation Bible school or day camp or—"

Pap held up one hand for silence while he dialed the phone number again.

"Yes, this is Alex Blossom," Pap said in a loud, professional voice. "I was calling in regard to a woman named Mary Cantrell—Mad Mary some folks call her around here. Perhaps you've heard tell of her."

Pap drew in a deep breath before he continued even more professionally.

"Sir, I have reason to believe that Mary Cantrell has met with an accident and that's why I'm calling you—to find out if that's true."

There was another pause. Pap said, "No, she wouldn't claim me as family, but I'm as close a friend as she's got in the world. I live out her way."

Again Pap listened. "Yes, I'll hold," he said.

Then Pap put one hand over the receiver and turned to Junior. "They're checking for me."

Junior said, "Can I go on about the surprise while we wait?"

"Yes, go on about the surprise."

Mad Mary lay without moving. Her eyes were closed. Her breathing was shallow.

Her mind was a blank.

Then slowly there appeared on the blank screen of her

50

mind a shape that had been on the ceiling of her bedroom when she was a girl. She hadn't seen that shape in sixty-five years, yet she knew it at once.

She had been afraid of that shape as a girl. That brown shape had been the first thing she had ever feared in her life.

"It's just a water stain," her mother had told her. "It's bled through the paint on the ceiling."

"But it keeps coming back," she'd said. "Why does it keep coming back? We've painted the ceiling and painted the ceiling. If it's just a stain, why does it keep coming back?"

"There's probably a leak in the attic roof. I'll have it patched."

But even after the roof had been patched and the ceiling painted with two coats of indoor enamel, the stain was still there.

"It's in your mind," her mother had said then. "And you are not to mention it again."

That's where it was now for sure—in Mary's mind. It had bled through sixty-five years of time and there it was.

It wasn't a bear or a witch. It was scarier than that. It was a—a shape, a shape with long hairy arms that stretched out and fingers—no, talons—that would reach for her if she closed her eyes. That was what she could never make her mother understand, that if she closed her eyes . . .

Now, as she lay old and still, too tired to open her eyes, the shape bled into her mind the way it had bled through two coats of paint on her ceiling.

The shape was becoming clearer now, taking on real form. The talons were growing longer, reaching out.

Mary drew in a ragged breath through her pale lips—
she recognized the shape at last. At last it was clear.

The brown shape, the shape that wouldn't go away, the
shape that was almost touching her with its cold talons,
that shape was the angel of death.

Chapter Nine

The Tunnel of Doom

MUD WAS ON THE FRONT PORCH. FROM TIME TO TIME HE
shook himself vigorously. That's what a morning in the
basement did to him, left him with the need to shake it off.

There were only three things to do in the basement,
and these all had to be done on the top step—howl, try to
dig through the door, and smell the crack beneath the
door to see if anybody had come home to let him out.

Mud shook again.

He scratched behind his left ear in a place that had been
itching for twenty minutes. He shook himself again.

Moving across the porch, he flopped down in the patch
of sunlight by the steps. He rolled over onto his back and
twisted from side to side. A low moan of pleasure came
from him as the rough boards scratched his back where it
always itched.

He lay still for a moment, his body curled into a C,
letting the sun warm his stomach. That done, he rolled

over and dropped his head onto his paws. His long ears flowed like velvet over his legs.

A breeze blew from the pine trees. Mud inhaled the pleasant and familiar smells so different from the musty air of the basement—the earth still damp from yesterday's rain, the squirrels, the . . .

There was something new in the air.

Mud opened his eyes. He lifted his head, his long nose pointing toward the pines.

The look in Mud's yellow eyes sharpened. He got to his feet. His tail began to sweep the porch floor behind him like a broom.

He inhaled again and his tail stopped in mid-wag. Mud stood at the edge of the steps for a moment, statue still. The breeze had died, but the scent lingered in the still October air.

This scent was strange, mysterious. It was animal and yet no animal that Mud knew of. The possibilities drew him forward.

But just as he was ready to go down the steps and investigate, he saw something happening in the pine trees.

This was something Mud did not understand. Mud lowered himself to his haunches.

Mud watched with his brows drawn together, his ears pulled back, his golden eyes shining.

Pap was still waiting for the policeman to come back to the phone so Junior asked, "Do you want me to go on about the tunnel or be quiet?"

"What?"

"Pap! The tunnel! The tunnel!"

"Yes, Junior, tell me about the tunnel, but the minute the policeman comes back to the phone . . ."

"I'll shut up," Junior promised. He leaned forward over his elbows.

"The tunnel's got rooms at each end—one's a dining room, one's a bedroom. The bedroom has soft grass in it for a bed and the dining room's got seeds for—"

Pap held up his hand for silence.

He listened. "Yes, sir, I'm still on the line." Then Pap said, "No record of anything, huh?"

Pap's hand was up, forbidding speech, so Junior waited.

"Well, I appreciate your checking for me. And let me leave my name and number just in case." Pap hung up the phone reluctantly.

"Pap, I think it's good news that they don't know anything. It's when they *do* know something, that it's bad. She hasn't been in a wreck. She's not dead. There are a lot of things to be grateful for."

"I guess, but I sure will feel better when I know where she's at."

"I will too."

"Well, we haven't got anything to do but wait, so why don't you go on about your tunnel or surprise or whatever it is."

Pap kept his hands on the phone, drumming his fingers as if he wanted it to ring.

"You're sure you want me to tell you?"

"Go on with it, Junior."

"I'll stop the minute the phone rings."

"I'd appreciate it."

"Here goes," Junior said.

Mud crossed the yard.

He stood looking curiously down at the boards that

56

jagged across the pine needles. His ears pointed forward. His look sharpened.

He moved silently along the boards, sniffing. The scent was getting stronger now. It was animal. Mud's nose was wet with excitement. Mud loved to hunt.

Mud scratched one board and it flipped over, revealing a small ditch. Mud put his nose into the excavation and inhaled. Mud smelled an unfamiliar smell. This caused his excitement to increase.

He flipped over another board.

Stronger scent. More excitement.

He moved along the tunnel fast now, nose pushing aside boards as he went, paws digging, pine needles flying out behind him.

With the speed of lightning he continued down the line of boards, his look intent, his ears high. When there was only one board left, Mud pounced.

"So, Pap, that's what I was doing all day yesterday— making a tunnel. Will you come see it now? It's the most wonderful tunnel in the entire world."

"Well, give me a minute. Let me get up."

Pap stood up in three stages. First he stood in a stoop. Then his back straightened. Then his legs.

"Hurry, Pap."

"You can't hurry old legs," Pap said.

"If I don't show someone my tunnel soon, I'm going to bust wide open!"

"Well, I wouldn't want that to happen."

At last Mud was satisfied. He straightened. His eyes shone.

He lifted his leg on the upended boards. He scratched

57

vigorously with his hind legs, sending dirt and pine needles and grass flying into the air behind him.

Then, mission accomplished, with his tail as high as a flag of victory, Mud headed for the house.

Chapter Ten

Death in the Afternoon

PAP WAS STILL WAITING FOR THE LAST STAGE OF HIS
stand—the straightening of his legs—to take place, so he
spoke from a stoop.

"Wait a minute. Let me get this straight, Junior. The
school hamster was in that cage."

"Yes!"

Junior couldn't help himself. He smiled. At last he had
Pap's attention. And not only his attention! Pap was getting to his feet to see the tunnel. He was even willing to
leave the phone for a few minutes.

"You made a tunnel and you put the school hamster in
it?"

"Yes!"

"This was what you were doing yesterday?"

"Yes!"

"When did you put him in there?"

"Yes!" Junior was on such a roll of yeses that he couldn't

stop himself. "I mean, I put him in when I got home from school. I couldn't decide whether to put him in the bedroom or the dining room, but I finally chose the bedroom and I think that was the right choice. He was probably tireder than he was hungry. You can't believe how happy he was."

Junior remembered a phrase his mother used sometimes that fit the occasion. "Pap, he lit up like a Christmas tree!"

"Junior, you are responsible for that hamster."

"I know! I love being responsible for him! I didn't know how much fun it would be to be responsible."

"That's one of the reasons teachers do these things—to teach you responsibility."

"And it does, Pap. I'm—I don't know—I'm more responsible than I ever thought I could be. I couldn't be any more responsible if I tried."

"When you're responsible for something, Junior, you don't leave it unattended."

Pap had now straightened all the way and was looking down at Junior sternly from his full height.

"It's not unattended," Junior said.

"Who's watching it? Vern and Michael?"

"Nobody. That's the beauty of it. It's watching itself. I mean, it's covered with boards—many, many boards. He can't get out, Pap. This is the nicest little tunnel anybody ever made. He was so happy to get— Pap, wait for me!"

Junior followed Pap through the living room. Something about the fast way Pap was moving made a feeling of dread creep into his happiness.

Junior knew nothing had happened—nothing could have happened to a tunnel like his. It was absolutely escape-proof.

Still, a small dark cloud had appeared directly over the tunnel. Junior needed to see his tunnel to send it away.

On the porch, Junior passed Pap. He paused beside Mud who was scratching a flea behind his left ear.

"Is that your tunnel yonder?" Pap asked, pointing toward the pines.

Junior shielded his eyes with one hand.

He didn't answer. His arm began to tremble. A chill touched the back of his neck.

For Junior saw the destruction. His hand dropped. Both hands closed, prayerlike, over his heart.

Boards were everywhere. The boards he had laid with such care and pride. These boards had been tossed about as if by a tornadic force of nature. The exposed tunnel was a dark scar on the earth.

"Pap!" Junior breathed the word with such horror that Pap put one hand on his shoulder.

"Now, now, don't get your tail in a knot until we see what's happened."

"Pap!"

They went down the steps and started across the yard together. Junior tried to break into a run, but his legs weren't strong enough.

"Now, now," Pap said. "Maybe it's not as bad as it looks."

But Junior knew it was worse.

He ran, rubber-legged, and got to the trees first. He began picking up the boards, looking under each one.

"Pap!" Each time he said the word, there was more horror in it.

"Where is he, Pap? Where's Scooty?"

"It don't look like he's here."

"What happened? What happened?"

61

Now Junior was clutching his chest the way Pap had clutched his when he had his heart attack.

Pap scratched his head. "Well . . ."

"But what could have happened? When I left—and that was just ten or fifteen minutes ago, Pap—when I left him, all the boards were in place. Everything was perfect. There was not one single, single crack in one single board . . ."

Junior moved around the disaster area, examining overturned boards. Tears of misery began to roll unnoticed down his cheeks.

"What happened?"

"Junior, Junior, Junior," Pap said. "You don't put a hamster in a tunnel like that."

"Where is he? We've got to find him. Please, please help me find him."

Junior was flipping over boards he had flipped over two or three times before. He muttered with increasing apprehension, "Not here, not here. Where is he, Pap? Please help me find him. I'm responsible for this animal. If I don't find him, Pap, I can never go to school again, never."

"You have to go to school, Junior."

"Not if I don't find him. Help me, Pap!"

Junior broke off and drew in his breath. He bent to inspect a piece of wood. "Pap, there's dog pee on this board."

Pap braced one hand on his back and leaned over to take a look. As if he saw the direction Junior's mind was taking he said, "Now, Junior, you don't know that's dog pee."

"And those are dog scratch marks!"

"Junior," Pap took his shoulder, "now don't go jumping to conclusions."

Junior shook him off. "And, look, Pap. There is a paw print. Right there by the bedroom! And it's a dog paw print. And it's a big one. It's Mud's, not Dump's."

Junior lifted his eyes from Scooty's empty bedroom and looked at the porch. Mud lay at the edge of the steps in the afternoon sun, licking his leg.

Junior's eyes narrowed to slits. His heart turned to stone.

He said one word, and that one word was a cold, hard, unforgiving accusation.

"Mud."

Chapter Eleven

Dirty Rotten Murderer

"DIRTY ROTTEN MURDERER!"

"Now, Junior . . ."

"Dirty rotten murderer, come out from under there so I can murder you. See how it feels to be murdered! See how you like it!"

At the first cry of "Dirty rotten murderer!" Mud had been on the porch. He stopped licking his leg and looked up, interested.

At the second "Dirty rotten murderer!" he lowered his ears and watched Junior's long staggering charge toward the porch.

At the third "Dirty rotten murderer!" he did the only sensible thing for a dog to do. He slipped down the steps and disappeared under the porch.

He had paused for a moment in the cool shadows of the steps to make sure the cry had been directed at him.

When Junior's face, distorted with anger, had appeared, he retreated behind an old truck tire.

Junior tried to crawl in after Mud, but Pap held on to his ankles. "Now, now," Pap said. "Hold on."

"Let go of me! Let go of me! I'm going to kill that dirty rotten murderer if it's the last thing I do."

Mud decided to retreat farther. He moved behind the apple crate and lay down to see what was going to happen next.

Mud's vocabulary consisted of eight words—*no, supper, go, bath, ride, possum, walk,* and *stay.* He loved to hear *supper, go* (especially when it was preceded by *let's*), *ride, possum,* and *walk.* He hated *no, bath,* and *stay.*

But Mud also knew tone of voice. And the tone of voice in which "Dirty rotten murderer" had been thrown at him was not good.

Mud, ears down, listened to the commotion at the edge of the house—Junior's screams, Pap's attempts to soothe.

After a while, Mud got tired and he curled up behind the apple crate for a long wait.

"Push us, Ralphie! Give us a push!"

Ralphie's brothers were calling from inside a Maytag cardboard box. The new washing machine had arrived that morning; and as soon as it had been unloaded, the brothers claimed the box.

They were now poised at the top of the hill in the side yard, begging to be pushed over the top.

"Mom'll be home any minute," Ralphie said, glancing at the street.

"No! No! She won't be back till after lunch!"

His brothers' voices, muted by cardboard, rose with enthusiasm.

65

"You're sure?"

"We promise."

"Well, I won't push you—"

"P-LLLLEASE."

"I won't push you, but I'll get you right to the edge and you can do the rest. That way you'll be pushing yourselves, all right?" Ralphie thought this might come in handy later, as an alibi, if the downhill plunge didn't end happily.

"All right!"

Ralphie worked the Maytag box to the crest of the hill and stepped back. "Okay!" he shouted. "You can push yourselves if you want to. I can't stop you."

The Maytag box came alive as the brothers worked to get it over the top of the hill. There was a long moment while the box paused in midair. The brothers screamed with anticipation.

Then the box went over.

And as it plunged down the hill, end over end, Ralphie's mother's station wagon turned into the drive.

Ralphie stepped back, holding up his hands to show he had had no part in the activity.

The station wagon would have hit him if Ralphie had not jumped out of the way. "Mom!"

Ralphie's mother leaped out in her clown suit. "Ralphie, if your brothers are in that box, your life as a happy person is over!"

"Dirty rotten . . ."

Junior was still at it.

"Junior . . . Junior."

So was Pap. Pap was stroking the top of Junior's head in

a soothing way, as if he were trying to peak his hair into a cap, but Junior didn't even feel the pats.

"Junior . . . Junior . . . Junior . . ." Pap said, but Junior was so far gone he couldn't hear his own name.

In a firmer tone Pap said, "Junior, stop yelling and listen to me."

Junior shook his head from side to side in silent, violent refusal.

"Junior, now you don't know he did it."

Maggie had come home from school by this time, and she was sitting on the steps eating a banana.

"Oh, Pap," Maggie said. "Face the facts. Your precious Mud ate Scooty. Mud had pine needles in his fur and dirt on his nose."

Pap didn't answer.

In the silence that followed, Junior threw back his head and wailed, "Sthcoo-oo-ooty." He had been crying so long that his nose was stopped up, and he could no longer talk right.

"Junior, stop howling," Maggie said sensibly. "We'll go to the mall tomorrow and get another hamster. All hamsters look alike."

"No, they d-dunt. They dunt!"

"Oh, all right, they dunt," Maggie said.

Maggie threw her braids behind her shoulder and stretched out her legs.

"I remember when I was in second grade we had a class guinea pig named Gimpy and Jimmy Lee Atkins took him home for the Christmas holidays and when Gimpy came back he was a different color."

"Don't talk!" Junior said.

Maggie went on calmly. "Jimmy Lee claimed he had

67

used his Dad's Grecian Formula comb on Gimpy by mistake, but—"

"I asked you not to talk!"

Junior couldn't bear to hear ordinary conversation, as if nothing had happened, when his whole world had come to an end.

"Junior, you have got to accept the fact that Scooty is gone, and that yelling at Mud is not going to bring him back."

At that, a wave of anguish washed over Junior so great that he banged his head against the side of the house.

"Dirty (thunk) rotten (thunk) murderer (THUNK)."

He never even felt any pain.

"Stop that, Junior, you're going to give yourself a headache," Maggie said.

Maggie was used to taking a motherly role with Junior. She'd been doing it since the day he was born.

One time last year she'd seen a picture in her geography book—they were studying Asia—and the picture had been of real young girls carrying babies on their backs. She had looked at the picture and she had remembered the feel of Junior's tiny hands around her neck because that was the exact way she had carried him.

"Junior . . . Junior," Pap said. He slid one hand to Junior's forehead to protect it from future blows. "Junior, give it up."

"I won't give it up! I'll never give it up. Never! Never! Never!"

Chapter Twelve

Boys in a Box

"No, Ralphie!"

"Mom, please."

"I said NO!"

"Mom, I've got to go to the Blossoms. I promised."

"You are going one place—to your room. You are grounded for the rest of the month."

"Why? What did I do?"

"You almost killed your brothers. You pushed them off a cliff in a Maytag box."

"I didn't."

"I saw you."

"Mom, listen, you couldn't have seen me push them because I didn't do it. Ask them if you don't believe me."

"Did I push you guys?" Ralphie called down the hill. "Tell the truth."

Ralphie didn't wait for the truth. He lowered his voice confidentially. "Mom, they asked me to push them; they begged me. But I said 'No.' I said, 'You'll get hurt.' Mom, they said, 'We won't get hurt. We promise.' I still said 'No.'

"So they said, 'Just move us to the edge, Ralphie. Just to the edge.' I said, 'What good would that do?'

"They said, 'If we have to move ourselves, we can't see where we're going and we might topple over before we're ready. Then we really could get hurt.'

"That made sense and, Mom, you know me—Mr. Nice Guy—I moved them very carefully to the edge. I said, 'You're sure you want to do this?' They said, 'We're sure!' I stepped back. I said, 'Don't blame me if you hurt yourselves.' They said, 'We won't!' and over they went. If anybody ought to be punished, it's them!"

His mom didn't even look at him. Her eyes watched the brothers.

"Also, Mom," Ralphie continued, "I had absolutely no idea that a mere Maytag box could . . ."

Ralphie trailed off. He had watched the Maytag box, containing his brothers, with real awe, and Ralphie was not easily awed. Ralphie hadn't known it was possible for a Maytag box to actually exceed the speed limit.

That box had gone eighty miles an hour. It could have won the Indy 500. If it hadn't run into the Wilsons' azaleas, it would still be going. It would be on the freeway, passing eighteen-wheelers.

Ralphie had been so astonished that he had not noticed his mother drive up. When he finally did look, he immediately held up both hands to show he had had no part in the event. His mother was in her clown suit because she had just returned from a balloon delivery—but clown makeup could not hide her displeasure.

She joined him in time to see the Maytag box come to rest against the azaleas. Then there was a long pause.

Ralphie and his mother were frozen in place, neither wanting to go down the hill and find damaged bodies.

The Maytag box came to life. It wiggled. It spoke. "Let's do it again!"

"Yeah!"

Only then, after he was sure his brothers were safe— only then, to his credit—did he say, "Well, I'm going to the Blossoms."

Was his mom grateful for his good grace in waiting to see if his brothers were alive? No. Her displeasure worsened and turned to fury. If there was one thing worse than a displeased clown, it was an angry one.

Ralphie was glad Maggie was not here to see his mom as a full-blown ogress or Maggie might have resented even more her label as ogrette.

His brothers were halfway up the hill now, pulling the box behind them, ready for another run. "I want to do it by myself this time," one was saying. "Then you can do it by yourself, all right?"

"Then we BOTH—"

Ralphie's mother cut short their plans as she had cut short Ralphie's.

"Give me that box!"

She took a few steps down the hill, reached the rest of the way, and tried to grab it from their hands.

"What are you doing?" they cried, so startled they slipped back down the hill and out of reach.

"And if I ever catch you in another Maytag box I'm going to Maytag you!"

The brothers weren't worried about being Maytaged. Their mom used a lot of brand names for threats. "When I find out which one of you ate the Krispy Kremes, I'm going to Krispy Kreme you!" She had, on different occa-

71

sions, threatened to Rice Krispie them, Pepperidge Farm them, even Sara Lee them. They were worried about losing the box. Boxes this strong didn't come along every day.

"Mom, that's not fair," they said. "Dad told us we could have the box."

"I'll give you the box, all right." She got her hands on the box and began to wrest it from them.

In a mature voice, speaking as if it were the first time he had said this, Ralphie said, "Mother, I'll be going to the Blossoms now."

"Ralphie!" She spoke through clenched teeth. She wouldn't even look at him. "I do not want to hear one more word out of you. Is that clear?"

Ralphie nodded.

"Then answer me!"

"Yes, it's clear."

"Then go on. Get out of here."

"You're sure?"

"Yes, I'm sure. And don't come back till dark. I'm sick of the sight of all of you."

"Thanks, Mom."

Ralphie got on his bike and pedaled for the Blossoms' farm.

Behind him, his mom gained possession of the box and the brothers and began swatting them. So, this time the threat had been carried out. She was Maytaging them.

Ralphie pedaled faster.

There was one thing on Ralphie's mind—the flower. That flower. The flower he had put in Maggie's braid.

He didn't know the botanical name for it—it could be an unnamed weed for all he knew—still, to Ralphie, it was the most important flower there had ever been in the world.

Ralphie saw that flower as a symbol of his and Maggie's whole relationship, their whole future relationship.

What had Maggie done with that flower?

If, his thinking went, she had thrown it in the trash can or down the toilet or down the disposal—that was one thing. But suppose, just suppose, she had kept it. Suppose that while she was combing her hair, getting ready for bed, just suppose that while she was doing this, she had taken the flower and put it on top of her jewelry box!

The thought made Ralphie's heart race. He had never been in her bedroom, had never seen her dresser. He didn't even know if she had a jewelry box. But if she did have one and if there were a flower on top of it—that flower, THE flower—then she was as much in love with him as he was with her.

So Ralphie wasn't pedaling toward the Blossom farm. He was pedaling toward a flower and the answer to the most important question of his life.

Mud lifted his head. The yard was silent. He got up, stretched, shook, and peered around the apple crate.

As he started out, he paused to lift his leg on the old truck tire. He stretched again.

He ducked under the bathroom pipes, but paused to let them scratch his back, just above the tail on the spot that always needed scratching. Then he proceeded toward the steps.

He was moving into the sunlight when there was a sudden lunge in his direction. It was Junior.

Mud didn't pause to question why Junior was jumping at him, why Junior was twisting his fingers in his bandana, why Junior was screaming, "Dirty rotten murderer. Now I got you, you filthy double-dirty rotten murderer."

With one deft twist, Mud was out of his bandana and out of Junior's grasp. He went back behind the apple crate, in a crouch. He stood looking back at Junior for a moment, trying to puzzle it out.

Maggie said, "Junior, if you get your eyes all swollen up, Mom's going to be mad. She's not going to want the horse detective to see you with swollen eyes."

"I'm going to get that dog if it takes the rest of my life. You'll have to come out sometime, Mud, and when you do, you're going to get it!"

Mud watched Junior a moment more. Then he circled twice and dropped down in the dust, with his head resting on his paws, to wait for a more advantageous moment.

Chapter Thirteen

The Scariest Thing
in the World

MARY LAY WITHOUT MOVING. THE BED BENEATH HER
was hard, but it was not the good hard of the stone ledge
in her cave. The air she breathed was cool, but it was not
the natural cool of a cave. It was chemically cooled.

Her mind drifted from one unhappy comparison to another.

The noises were not the beautiful ones of nature—the
rustling of a vulture's wings, the calls of forest birds, the
faint rustle of a black snake in the corner of her cave.
These noises were man-made, metallic, unpleasant.

In the midst of these thoughts, something Junior had
once said drifted into her mind.

"You know what the scariest thing in the whole world
is?" he had asked.

"Well, I imagine that would vary," she had answered in
a conversational tone. "Some folks are scared of one thing;
some folks of another."

"Yes, but—"

"For example, some people would be scared to spend the night in a cave, Junior, and I do that every night of my life. Some people would be scared of vultures, and they're my good friends."

"Mine too, but I'm talking about the scariest thing that can happen to anybody! Anybody! You! Me! The President of the United States! Anybody!"

"What's that, Junior?"

Junior had put so much feeling into his words that he had to swallow before he could speak.

"The scariest thing in the whole world," he went on, "is waking up and not knowing where you are."

He paused to let the truth of his words sink in. Then he added, "It's happened to me two times." He held up two dirty fingers for emphasis. "So I know."

"It never has happened to me, but I can see how it would be scary."

Even though Mad Mary was at least sixty years older than Junior, she sometimes felt they were the same age.

"Very scary."

"You want to tell me about it, Junior?"

Junior nodded. "I wouldn't mind."

"Well, one time I was right here in your cave." Junior and Mad Mary were in the cave at the time of this conversation, so Junior pointed to the very spot—the ledge.

"You took me out of the coyote cage and brought me here while I was asleep. You put me right there and I woke up and it was so dark I thought I'd gone blind. I felt all around me and I felt stones and blankets and I didn't recognize those stones and blankets and I got up and I started crying and my crying didn't even sound like my crying. I got scareder and scareder and I started across the cave and I fell and I bit my lip and I tasted blood. I screamed and screamed and I would have kept on screaming but I felt your shoe . . . you probably don't remember this."

"Oh, yes. I remember."

"You do?"

"You're the only person that was ever in my cave. I'm not likely to forget anything about your visits."

"Really?"

Junior appeared to be distracted by the compliment, so Mary said, "Go on, go on."

"You know the rest."

"I'd like to hear your side of it."

"I felt your shoe and I thought it was Pap's; you wear the same kind of shoes."

"Brogans."

Junior nodded. "It was so, so dark, and then you struck a match and I looked up and saw—"

Junior broke off. Mary had seen that he was reluctant to describe what he had seen. Her face wasn't a pretty sight under the best conditions, and lit up by a match in a strange cave—well, children didn't call her a witch for nothing.

She remembered that Junior's eyes had rolled up into his head and he had fainted, which was probably the best thing that could have happened to him.

To change the subject, she said, "There was another time you woke up and didn't know where you were?"

"Oh, yes. Well, the other time it happened—waking up and not knowing where I was—you know where I was?"

"No."

"In the hospital!"

77

"Was that when you fell off the barn and broke both your legs?"

"Yes! And I was just lying there with my eyes shut and, Mary, when I was little I used to be able to see through my eyelids. I really could do it. Nobody believes me but I could. One time our teacher told us to close our eyes so we could pretend something and I closed mine and through my eyelids I saw her adjust her brassiere. That really happened."

"I believe you."

"Anyway, this time I couldn't see through my eyelids and all I knew was that I was somewhere I really and truly didn't want to be!"

"I imagine that was scary."

"I told you." Junior nodded wisely. "It's the scariest thing in the whole world."

As Mary relived that conversation, she knew a deep kinship with Junior. Tears squeezed through her closed eyelids.

As usual, Junior had spoken the truth that day. Waking up and not knowing where you are is the scariest thing that can happen to a person. She knew it for a fact, because now it had happened to her.

She knew three things about this place even without opening her eyes. It was somewhere she had never been before in her life. It was somewhere she had never wanted to be. It was somewhere she wanted to get out of.

She tried to raise her hand to her face. She felt so strange—all the strange sounds, strange smells, strange surroundings made her want to feel her features and make sure they were the same.

Her hands wouldn't raise. They were tied. She was tied

down! Wherever she was, someone had tied her down so she couldn't get out.

Mad Mary couldn't put it off any longer. Mad Mary decided to open her eyes.

"I'll never give it up. Never! Never Never!"

Pap said gently, "Can't you forgive the dog, Junior?"

Junior shook his head.

"Will you do it for me? For Pap?"

Again Junior shook his head.

"We don't know that he did it," Pap argued gently. "We'll probably never know for sure."

"We could cut him open with a butcher knife," Junior suggested.

Junior was still on his knees, glaring into the depths under the house. He had Mud's bandana wrapped around his wrist.

"Junior, if we get another hamster that looks exactly like Scooty, will you forgive Mud?" Maggie asked from the steps.

Junior shook his head. "No."

"Do you really honestly believe Mud killed Scooty?" Maggie asked.

Junior nodded.

"What about you, Pap?"

"Well, it don't look good for the dog—I admit that. But on the other hand, I ain't never known Mud to kill anything. If I point to a hole in the ground and say, 'Possum!' he'll dig, but he never caught one. He'll chase a squirrel until he's so tired he can't run another step, but he never caught one. When we catch fish I put them in the bucket and let him catch them, and he takes them in his mouth so

79

gently there ain't a tooth mark on them. Still . . . it don't look good for him now."

Maggie got up. She threw her braid behind her back in a purposeful way. "In cases like this, there's really only one thing to do."

"Yes!" Junior agreed. "Cut him open with a butcher knife."

"And what if Scooty's not inside?" Maggie said. "What are we going to do then—sew him back up and say, 'Sorry about that, Mud.' "

"I don't want any more talk about cutting my dog open," Pap said in a stern voice.

There was a pause while Junior stared sullenly under the house, and Pap stared disapprovingly at his back.

Pap turned his worried face to Maggie. "Go ahead, Maggie, what's your idea."

"Mud," Maggie said firmly, "has got to stand trial for murder."

Chapter Fourteen
Ralphie's Luck

RALPHIE LISTENED TO JUNIOR'S "I'LL NEVER GIVE IT UP" speech from the back porch of the Blossoms' house.

Apparently Mud had eaten a hamster, which was considered an act of murder. Ralphie couldn't have been more pleased. It took something like an act of murder to distract the Blossom family.

It was the Ralphie luck, he thought. The only time in his whole life that the Ralphie luck had deserted him was the time he had the accident on the riding lawn mower.

So now, with the family properly distracted, he could slip up the steps and into Maggie's bedroom—he knew which one it was because she often called out the window to him. "I'll be right down. Don't go away." As if he would.

Even with the Ralphie luck, Ralphie didn't take chances. He slunk down the hallway, close to the wall. He paused with his foot on the first step. He listened.

Maggie, Junior, and Pap were in the front yard. He

could hear their voices. Vern and Michael were at the side of the house—in the bushes. Ralphie had almost run into them, but they were laughing at some secret joke and never even saw him.

Ralphie's better judgment told him not to continue, but then his better judgment was always doing that. Ralphie started up the steps. He kept to the wall because he had read that was how thieves got up steps without being heard. Not one creaking board betrayed him.

In the upstairs hall, Ralphie paused.

Maggie's bedroom was on the right side of the stairs. As he crossed noiselessly to her room, his heart began to beat faster. He paused in the doorway to breathe the air in Maggie's room.

This air was different from any air Ralphie had ever breathed before. He felt that if he breathed enough of this splendid air, he would become intoxicated.

He had intended to go directly to the dresser and check for the flower, but the richness of the room overwhelmed him.

He stepped inside.

There were hundreds of pictures on the wall, and Ralphie moved around the room respectfully. He kept his hands behind his back as if he were in a museum.

Here was a snapshot of Maggie as a baby—coming home from the hospital. Ralphie leaned closer. She had on tiny cowboy boots instead of booties, and Mrs. Blossom, holding her, looked like a girl with a turned-up nose instead of a middle-aged woman.

Here was a birth announcement—Cotton and Vicki Blossom's baby girl, Maggie, has come out of the chute weighing seven pounds, two ounces. . . . Ralphie moved down the wall.

Here was a picture of her on a horse with a laughing man, her father. And here she was two years old maybe, holding a baby that had to be Vern. And here she and Vern were—maybe a year later—in cowboy outfits and hats.

And here she and Vern were holding Junior. It had to be Junior because Junior hadn't changed that much—same round face, round eyes. . . .

Ralphie heard a burst of anguish from Junior. Junior was now suggesting they cut Mud open with a butcher knife. Ralphie brought himself back to earth immediately.

Now. Where was the flower? He crossed to the dresser. In his mind the flower had been right there on top of the jewelry box, but there was no jewelry box.

Ralphie divided girls into two categories—girls (in little letters) and MAGGIE (in capitals). Girls would have jewelry boxes—MAGGIE would have what?

Where would a girl put a flower if she didn't have a jewelry box? Ralphie didn't have any sisters, and for the first time he regretted this.

The flower had to be here somewhere. He bent to look in the trash can. It wasn't there. That was good news.

Where did a MAGGIE keep things that had special meaning? Valuables, jewels, stuff like that.

There was a large basket full of barrettes and hair clips and ribbons. Ralphie stirred the contents with one finger to see if the flower could be concealed.

The more Ralphie stirred, the more fascinated Ralphie became with all these barrettes and hair things. There must be fifty, maybe a hundred, barrettes in this basket, barrettes from when Maggie was a baby. Here was a tiny little barrette shaped like a crayola, and here was a lady bug, cowboy boots, strawberries, and here was a rubber hair thing with marbles on the ends.

83

Ralphie stretched the elastic to see how it worked. He put it on his finger for a ring. Ralphie had never worn a ring before. The things they make to go in girls' hair, he thought, wondering at it.

Ralphie finished admiring his ring and looked down at the drawers. He wanted to open them but, of course, that would be prying.

He turned away. The nightstand. He crossed to Maggie's bed. No flower . . . no flower . . .

Ralphie heard a burst of laughter and moved to the side window. Vern and Michael were still down there, now holding their sides.

"Stop laughing!" Vern was saying.

"I can't. You're making me laugh."

"No, I'm not. You're making me laugh."

"Well, we can't go around the house until we stop laughing."

"I know but . . . but . . ."

Vern and Michael started laughing again. They made an effort to get themselves under control. They did this by looking down at their shoes.

Finally Vern said, "Are you ready?"

"Yes."

"You're sure?"

"Yes."

"You're sure you're not going to laugh?"

"Yes."

"Then let's go."

But before they could get around the corner of the house, they had started laughing again. "You did it that time," Vern accused when he was at last able to speak.

"I couldn't help it."

"Well, we have to help it."

"I know."

Vern wiped his eyes on the sleeve of his shirt. "Maybe if we think of something sad."

There was a pause.

Michael said, "I just thought of something sad."

"What?"

"Junior."

This one word caused them to collapse on the ground in such a fit of mirth Ralphie thought they were going to injure themselves. Finally they lay on their backs, too weak to move.

Ralphie turned away. Well, he had to face the fact that the flower was not here. He would just tidy up the dresser and go downstairs. He had spilled some of the barrettes.

On the porch below, Junior said. "Maggie's right."

Ralphie paused with barrettes in one hand to hear what Maggie had been right about.

"About what?" Pap asked for him.

"About putting Mud on trial for murder."

"Junior, what good will that do?"

"It's what happens to murderers. Did you hear that, Mud! You're going on trial for murder!"

Suddenly a prickly sense of unease came over Ralphie, as if an icy hand had touched him on the back of his neck. Before he could turn, a voice spoke from the doorway.

"And just what do you think you're doing?"

Ralphie lifted his eyes and met Maggie's in the mirror. Her eyes were as green and hard as mints.

He turned.

Maggie was standing in the doorway with her arms folded. The first thing Ralphie noticed was that she was no

85

longer an ogrette. Maggie had graduated with honors. Maggie was now a full-blown, adult-sized ogress.

For the second time in his life, the Ralphie luck had run out.

Chapter Fifteen

T-H-E Place

When Mad Mary opened her eyes, she found she was in the exact place she had feared she was. She was in a bed.

Mad Mary had not been in a bed in twelve years. She hadn't been under sheets either, or in a nightgown, or lit up by electric lights, or among strange people. She was all of those things now.

She knew where she was, but she didn't know how she had come to be here.

One moment she had been walking along between the woods and the road. She had a possum in her bag, her crook in her hand, and peace in her heart.

The next moment—anyway that was how it seemed— the next moment she was in a hospital bed with her hands tied to the railings.

"Oh, Junior." She sighed.

"She spoke!" a brisk voice announced. "She's awake.

88

Her eyes are open. I know you're awake. Can you hear me?"

Mad Mary closed her eyes.

Vern and Michael were now making their sixth attempt to go around the corner of the house. The first five tries had ended unsuccessfully with Vern and Michael, helpless with laughter, flopping around on the grass like fish just pulled from the creek.

"Now really and truly," Vern said, giving Michael a serious look. "Really and truly let's don't laugh this time."

"I won't if you won't."

"Wait, I've got it, I've got it," Michael said. "We'll go around and if we do laugh and they ask why, we'll say we can't tell because it might embarrass someone."

"Who?"

"Let me finish. If they make us tell, we'll say, 'Maggie and Ralphie up in a tree, k-i-s-s-i-n-g.' "

They laughed a little—it was like the hiccups now. The recovery of their backpacks had filled them with high spirits.

"Then Maggie will hit us—she always does—she hates for us to say that."

"But Maggie's in the house. I saw her go in."

"Well, then we'll do something else. If they ask why we're laughing, you say, 'Michael just told a joke,' and if they want to hear it, then I will tell the joke about the monkeys on Mars."

"Let's go."

The thought of the joke about the monkeys on Mars sobered Vern and Michael enough so they were able to come around the side of the house as serious as judges. They had both learned an important fact about humor—

something you should laugh at is never as funny as something you shouldn't.

"What's going on?" Vern asked innocently.

"Yeah, what's going on?" Michael echoed.

"Now, Mary, we know you're awake. We know you hear us. Open your eyes."

The woman's voice was firm, as if she was used to getting her way.

"Mary, can you hear me? Nod your head if you can."

Mary didn't want to, but she nodded.

"Now, Mary, we need some information for the records."

Mary was motionless under the strange stiff sheets. Her body felt stiff and strange too.

"We know your name. You're Mary Cantrell. You're a very famous person in this town, but nobody seems to know where you live. What is your address?"

Mad Mary shook her head from side to side, mute with misery.

"Can you remember your address?"

Mary shook her head.

"You can't remember your address?"

At last Mary spoke, her voice cracking from fear and lack of use. "I don't have one."

"You don't have an address. You're, like, homeless?"

Mary shook her head.

"You're not homeless."

"No."

"Where do you live then? What is your address?"

Mary saw it was no use now. She might as well give the woman what she wanted.

"I live," she said with great dignity, "in a cave."

*

Pap didn't look at Vern and Michael, who had just come around the corner of the house. He had Junior by the shoulders, forcing Junior to look at him. Junior didn't want to.

Pap said, "Junior, now if we have the trial and Mud is found innocent . . ."

"He won't be innocent. He's not innocent. How could he be innocent?"

"Everybody—even Mud—is innocent until proven guilty. That's the American way, Junior."

"Not Mud."

"Yes, even Mud. Now, Junior, if Mud is found innocent, then you'll accept that, won't you? You'll give up on taking your revenge?"

Silence.

"Junior?"

Silence.

"Junior, we can't have the trial unless you agree to abide by the results."

"Oh, all right. But he couldn't be found innocent because he's a dirty rotten murderer and everybody knows it. So there!"

Chapter Sixteen

Maggie and Ralphie

"AND JUST WHAT DO YOU THINK YOU'RE DOING?"

After Maggie said that, the silence in her bedroom stretched on and on until it was immeasurable in normal minutes and hours. Nothing could record the length of time Ralphie stood looking at Maggie and Maggie stood looking back with those mint-green eyes.

The silence was reaching the point where it could never be broken when Ralphie cleared his throat.

"I was looking for a Bible," he said.

The words were as astonishing to Ralphie as they were, apparently, to Maggie. But at least, Ralphie thought, he had the cool not to let his mouth drop open.

She was obviously incapable of even a "What?," so Ralphie repeated his statement in a courteous manner.

"I was looking," he paused effectively, "for a Bible."

The repetition of the words gave them the calm, steady ring of the truth.

Maggie's mouth remained open. She was still apparently in a state of shock.

"See, I heard you say you were going to have a trial," Ralphie went on with understated brilliance, "and you'll obviously need a Bible to swear in the witnesses. I was going to surprise you."

"Well, you certainly surprised me, all right."

Ralphie had surprised himself as well, but he didn't mention that.

Maggie came into the room. She scowled as she saw the barrettes in Ralphie's hand.

"You were looking for a Bible in my barrette basket?" she asked.

"I thought you might have one of those—er, pocket Bibles."

"No, I do not have a pocket Bible."

She crossed the room and held out her hand. Ralphie said, "Well, you can't blame me for hoping." He turned his hand over and deposited the barrettes in hers.

She looked them over with suspicion. Then with a sigh of dissatisfaction, she put them back in the basket.

The hair band with the marbles on it was still on Ralphie's ring finger. Ralphie worked it off, bent and pretended to pick it up for her.

"You missed one."

Maggie began straightening the objects on her dresser —even the ones he had not touched. She spent a lot of time getting everything just right.

Ralphie had the feeling Maggie was stalling for time, trying to figure out what was missing. Did she think he had come up here to steal barrettes or combs or hair ribbons? Still, he would rather she think that than that he had come up looking for a flower.

93

As far as he was concerned, Maggie was making too much over the fact that he looked for a pocket Bible in her barrette basket and spilled a few barrettes. If she hadn't had too many barrettes in the basket in the first place, he wouldn't have spilled anything.

All the barrettes and ribbons were back in the basket, the objects on the dresser were in perfect order, but Maggie still didn't look satisfied.

She looked around for something like a lid to slam on the basket for emphasis.

Maggie did not want to slam a lid on her barrette basket. She wanted to slam one on Ralphie's head.

Anyway, she wasn't looking for a lid. She was looking around to see if she could spot what Ralphie was doing in her bedroom. She knew he was up to something. What?

She couldn't ask him again, because that would give him the opportunity and satisfaction of being quick-witted. At one time she had admired Ralphie's quick wit, but "I was looking for a Bible" was too quick-witted.

"I didn't take anything, if that's what you're thinking," Ralphie said.

Maggie turned her green eyes on him, and Ralphie fell silent.

Maggie's eyes were her strong point, and she knew it. She could say a lot with her eyes, but she was mad enough now to use her voice too.

"You don't have to take something to commit a crime."

Ralphie waited. He shifted under her cool gaze.

"Trespassing is a crime, too, you know, and I don't think you can deny you're trespassing."

"Come on, Maggie, haven't we got enough crimes going on without making up something like trespassing? We've got a murder case on our hands."

"On OUR hands?"

Ralphie began the long walk to the door of Maggie's room. He limped a little, but she knew he was doing that to get her sympathy and it didn't work.

Halfway across the room, Ralphie said, "Oh, I just thought of something important."

Maggie didn't ask, but Ralphie told her anyway.

"I was wondering . . ." Ralphie moved into the hallway in a confident and manly way. Maggie watched his back with those hard green eyes.

At the stairs he turned. Maggie was still standing by the dresser.

"What I was wondering was . . ." Ralphie trailed off. He appeared to be listening to something. He smiled with secret satisfaction.

This secrecy of this smile was too much for Maggie. She crossed the room, grabbed the door, and slammed it shut in Ralphie's face.

"What I was wondering was—did anyone think to read Mud his rights?" Ralphie called through the closed door.

Of course she didn't answer, and after a moment she heard his footsteps going down the stairs.

Maggie stood at the door, breathing hard.

Slamming the door on Ralphie had helped ease her anger, but not enough. She walked to her bed. She threw back her covers. She flipped her pillow over. She looked down.

There was the flower Ralphie had worked into her braid the day before. She had slept on it. Her mother was always saying, "Whatever you put under your pillow,

95

you'll dream about. It's true, Shug, it works for me all the time."

So Maggie had put the flower under her pillow, and the only thing she had to be thankful for was that it hadn't worked. She had not dreamed about flowers or Ralphie or anything else that stupid.

She picked up the flower. She let it rest in her palm for a moment. It was wilted, unbearably soft. She crushed it in her hand and threw it in the trash can on her way to the door.

Chapter Seventeen
Mud in Absentia

MUD WOULDN'T COME OUT FROM BEHIND THE APPLE
crate for his trial.

"Make him come out, Pap," Junior demanded. "He's
your dog. He'll come out if you tell him to."

"Junior, it won't do one bit of good in this world to drag
that poor animal out here."

"It will!"

"Junior—"

Junior turned away from Pap and threw himself back
on his knees by the steps. He peered under the house.

"Mud, sup-per," he called with a false cheerfulness.
"Come on, Mud, I've got something real good for you."

"Don't lie to the dog."

Junior ignored Pap.

"Ride, Mud, want to go for a ride?"

Junior's head jerked up with sudden thought. He

looked over his shoulder at Maggie. "Will you do me a big, BIG favor?"

"What?"

"Go to the truck and blow the horn—one long, two shorts. That'll make him come out." One long, two shorts was Pap's signal to Mud that he was leaving and wanted Mud to go along.

"Leave my truck out of this," Pap said.

Ralphie was standing by the steps while all this was happening. His arms were crossed over his chest.

Ralphie had never felt so in control in his life. He was like a master puppeteer, he thought. He couldn't wait for the glorious moment when Maggie gave up her anger to recognize and appreciate his quick wit and clear thinking. He knew Maggie had not been serious when she slammed the door in his face, because when she came downstairs five minutes later, she had seemed perfectly normal.

"We'll have to try him in absentia," Ralphie said. He maintained a modest expression, which wasn't easy when his mouth kept saying brilliant things.

Junior turned to look at Ralphie. "What's that?" he asked.

Ralphie was happy to explain. "It's when the defendant is absent."

Junior looked to Pap for confirmation. Pap nodded. "That's what it is."

"So we can have the trial?"

"Yes."

"Right now?"

"Yes."

Junior got to his feet and dusted off his knees. "And we can sentence him and everything?"

"That's right."

"And carry it out?"

Ralphie said, "Mud will have to have representation."

Junior said, "What's that?"

"It's like a lawyer," Ralphie explained. "I'd like to defend Mud, since nobody else seems to want to."

Maggie stepped forward and gave him a cool glance. "I'll prosecute," she said.

"What's that?" Junior asked. His head was swiveling back and forth as if he were at a tennis match.

"That means Ralphie's going to try to prove Mud is innocent, and I am going to prove beyond a shadow of a doubt that Mud is guilty."

"Good," Junior said.

"Can we be the jury, me and Michael?" Vern asked. "Because we just came around the corner of the house—didn't we, Michael?—and we didn't hear anything and don't know what's going on."

"That's right," Michael said. "We'd make a good jury because we don't know anything."

"Will you be fair?" Maggie asked.

"Yes."

"Wait a minute, wait a minute, if we're going to have a trial here, let's do it right," Ralphie said. "We should choose a jury, the way they do in court."

Ralphie had already adopted his courtroom attitude, which, he had decided, would be unemotional, superior, and with a lot of law talk.

Maggie spoke without looking at him. "They are the only two people we have to choose from." Her voice was as icy as her eyes.

"It still wouldn't hurt to ask them a few questions. Also there ought to be some dogs on the jury."

"Dogs?"

99

"Yes, Mud is entitled to a jury of his peers. Where's Dump?"

"Last time I saw him, he was on the sofa," Maggie said.

"I'll get him," Junior said. He went in the house and came out with Dump in his arms. "Now, Dump," he was saying, "you're going to be on Mud's jury, and you know how mean Mud's been to you and—"

"That's influencing the jury," Ralphie said.

"It is not," Junior said. "I'm just talking to him. There!"

He handed Dump to Vern, and Vern put the dog between Michael and him. Dump looked from one boy to the other as if trying to figure out what was expected of him.

Pap said, "Somebody get me a hammer."

"What for?" Maggie asked.

"So I can bang it down on the porch railing and call this court to order."

Mad Mary's eyes were closed.

"Next of kin?" the woman asked.

No answer.

"Next of kin?"

Silence. Then with a low sigh, Mad Mary said, "My kinfolks are dead."

"All of them?"

"That's right."

"No living brothers or sisters?"

"No."

"No children?"

"No."

"I need the name of someone who could be notified in case of . . ." the woman trailed off.

100

". . . in case I die."

"You're not going to die, Mary, but we need to have this information. Could you give me the name of a friend?"

"Alex Blossom," she said.

Chapter Eighteen
The Trial

Junior was on the stand.

Junior had not actually been called to testify yet, but the presiding judge—Pap—had allowed him to take the stand anyway.

The witness stand was a folding lawn chair that had seen better days, and everytime Junior jiggled with anticipation the chair tipped.

The two attorneys, Maggie and Ralphie, were sitting opposite each other. Occasionally Ralphie would get Maggie's attention by saying, "Ms. Prosecuting Attorney," but she would never meet his eyes.

Mud, the defendant, was still in absentia under the porch. He had, now that everyone was letting him alone, fallen asleep.

Junior said, "Well, Pap, go ahead and say it."

"What?"

"Order in the court."

Pap rapped his hammer on the porch railing. "Order in the court."

The jury came to attention.

Maggie got briskly to her feet. She was determined to win this case even if it meant Mud would go to the electric chair.

"I'm ready with my opening statement," she said.

Pap said, "Proceed."

Ralphie said, "Sorry, for interrupting"—Ralphie's voice boomed out, a real courtroom voice—"but the judge forgot to ask how we plead, guilty or innocent."

Maggie shot Ralphie a look of pure hatred, but Ralphie shrugged. He had seen a lot of TV movies where opposing lawyers ended up madly in love, which is how he intended for this trial to end.

Pap sighed. "How do you plead?"

"Your honor, my client pleads not guilty—"

From the witness stand Junior interrupted with scorn. "Huh!"

". . . not guilty by reason of temporary insanity. The prosecuting attorney may proceed."

Maggie put her hands on her hips in what Ralphie thought was an unlawyerlike way. Her voice was also unlawyerlike. "It's not your place to tell me to proceed. You're not the judge."

"I stand corrected," Ralphie said with legal politeness. Ralphie was pleased with all his legalities. His politeness was as perfect as his courtroom voice, if he did say so himself.

Pap said, "Proceed! I'm not going to sit up here all afternoon." He struck the railing with the hammer so hard it left a dent in the wood.

103

"Gentlemen of the jury," Maggie said to Michael and Vern and Dump.

Now that the trial was under way, Michael and Vern had gotten interested and only had to give a rare thought to the monkeys on Mars.

Dump, unnoticed by the other members of the jury or the attorneys, lay down, put his head on Vern's leg, and closed his eyes.

"Gentlemen, this afternoon I have the unpleasant job of asking you to convict a dog of willful, premeditated murder. The evidence is overwhelming. I call my first witness —Junior Blossom."

Junior twitched with eagerness, causing his lawn chair to tip dangerously. "I'm here."

"Er, your honor," Ralphie said, "I appreciate the prosecutor's zeal, but I'd like a chance to make MY opening statement."

"Make it."

"Thank you, your honor."

Maggie's back was to him, which was unfortunate because Ralphie wanted her to see what a masterful opening statement he was going to make. However, she couldn't turn off her ears. Ralphie had never fully appreciated that about ears before. She would have to hear every single brilliant word of it.

"Gentlemen of the jury, at this moment my client lies cowering under the house . . ."

"Sleeping's more like it," Maggie muttered to the jury.

Michael and Vern snickered. Ralphie ignored them. Dump slept on.

". . . lies cowering under the house—afraid to come out because he is no longer part of the family who once loved him. He is a dog with a broken heart, a dog who was driven into temporary insanity by the presence of a hamster carelessly left unattended in a poorly constructed—"

Junior gasped and swiveled around in the lawn chair. "Pap, is he allowed to say that?"

Pap didn't break the rhythm of his rocking. "You'll get your turn, Junior."

"I repeat," Ralphie went on, "carelessly left unattended. My client, driven temporarily insane, did what any dog would do. Dogs are known to be driven temporarily insane by hamsters in poorly made tunnels. So what my client is really accused of this afternoon is of simply being a dog. So, gentlemen of the jury, this afternoon I'm going to prove that the real guilt lies not with the dog, who was merely being true to his nature, but with that boy on the witness stand waiting to testify against him!"

There was a stunned silence as Ralphie pointed to the startled Junior.

Ralphie said, "Thank you, your honor."

Chapter Nineteen

Verdict!

"Have you reached a verdict?" Pap asked.

"No, we haven't reached a verdict. Pap, we can't reach a verdict until we go somewhere and talk about it," Vern said.

"Well, go on, but be quick. I've had about enough of this foolishness. I need to call the police again."

"Come on, Michael. Wake up, Dump, you've got to come too. You're the peer."

Michael and Vern and Dump disappeared around the corner of the house. Three long minutes went by.

Ralphie spent the time looking at Maggie. Maggie spent the time ignoring Ralphie. Junior spent the time on the witness stand.

Junior was no longer twitching with eagerness. All his eager twitches had gone out of him in that terrible moment when Ralphie had pointed at him and cried, "The real guilt lies not with the dog, who was merely being true

to his nature, but with that boy on the witness stand waiting to testify against him!"

Junior had never liked people to point at him and say
ugly things. After that, Junior could not enjoy the trial no
matter how hard he tried.

He was still on the stand, in the witness chair, because
he had been unable to move even when he was excused.

All Junior wanted now was to go home. The trouble was
he was home.

He hadn't known how terrible it would make him feel
to be a witness, and he hadn't had the pleasure of seeing
others go through the same discomfort because he had
been the only witness.

First Maggie had questioned him and he hadn't even
enjoyed that.

"And where was Mud when you came out of the
house?"

"On the porch."

"What was he doing?"

"Scratching."

"Did you notice anything unusual about him?"

"He had dirt on his nose and pine needles in his fur."

"Was this the same kind of dirt found at the scene of the
murder?"

"Yes."

"And were these the same kind of pine needles found at
the scene of the murder?"

"Yes."

"Did you notice anything at the scene of the crime to
lead you to believe Mud had been there?"

"Yes."

"What did you notice?"

"A paw print and some dog pee."

108

"And this paw print was the same size as Mud's?"

"Yes."

"Objection, your honor," Ralphie said. "Since the defendant is under the house and there is no way to prove the size of his paw—"

"Objection overruled," Pap said. "I seen the paw print and it was Mud's."

Maggie said, "Thanks, Pap," before she turned to Ralphie. "Your witness."

Junior had liked it even less when Ralphie had cross-examined.

"So, Junior, you testified that there was dirt on the defendant's nose."

"Yes."

"Was it unusual for the defendant to have dirt on his nose?"

"Well . . ."

"Had you ever seen the defendant with dirt on his nose before?"

"Yes, but . . ."

"Just answer the questions, please. Had you ever seen the defendant with dirt on his nose before?"

"Yes."

"Had you ever seen the defendant with pine needles in his fur before?"

"Well . . ."

"Answer the question, please."

"Yes."

"As a matter of fact, isn't it true that the defendant usually had dirt on his nose, that he usually went around with pine needles in his fur?"

"Maybe."

"Answer the question, Junior," Pap said.

"Oh, all right."

"Isn't it also true that you knew Mud was frequently in the pine trees?"

"I guess so."

"You knew this and yet you deliberately built a tunnel where you knew the dog would go and you built the tunnel in such a shoddy manner that any dog could overturn it?"

"It was not shoddy. You saw it, Pap. It was perfect before Mud ruined it."

"Answer the question, please."

"No!"

Now there was quiet in the yard. The questions, the summations were over. Both Maggie and Ralphie had rested their cases.

The jury had now been out for five minutes, and everyone in the yard was beginning to get restless.

Then Vern and Michael came around the corner of the house in a burst of enthusiasm. They had spent their time not deliberating the verdict but practicing to say it in unison.

Michael was muttering, "Now don't give it away. I saw this on TV. If you look at the defendant that means the verdict is innocent. If you keep your eyes down, it means guilty."

"We can't look at the defendant. He's still under the house."

"Well, don't give it away."

Dump was in Vern's arms. He looked rested. The three of them took their places in the jury box.

"Gentlemen, have you reached a verdict?" Pap asked in a tired voice.

110

"We have!"

"What is the verdict?"

"We find the defendant—"

They said this in perfect unison, but they didn't get to finish.

For at that moment, Vicki Blossom's truck drove into the courtroom.

Chapter Twenty

A Terrible Mist

VICKI BLOSSOM LEAPT FROM THE TRUCK.

"I am furious! Furious! I could scream with fury. Guess what?"

Maggie said, "Mother—"

"I have looked forward to this weekend and looked forward to this weekend and now somebody up in Virginia has murdered a horse."

Maggie said, "Speaking of murder, Mom, we are right in the middle of a murder trial ourselves. Your truck is blocking the courtroom."

"I think I can wrap our trial up," Ralphie said in a matter-of-fact voice. "I was just getting ready to approach the bench."

"Approach the bench!" Maggie swirled around. "What for?"

Pap was trying to get out of his rocking chair, but his knees weren't cooperating.

"Your honor, I would like to introduce a new and startling piece of evidence."

Maggie said, "Ralphie, you are really getting on my nerves. You are the one who wanted everything to be so legal. The jury is back in! They are giving their verdict! You have no right to introduce anything, much less new evidence!"

"I beg the prosecuting attorney's indulgence," Ralphie said with a slight, legal bow. Ralphie was glad to see that shut her up.

"I need only one moment, your honor," Ralphie told Pap. He went up the steps and into the house.

Inside, Ralphie broke into a grin. He loved it. He loved it. It couldn't be better.

As soon as he had seen Vern and Michael and their helpless laughter from Maggie's bedroom window, he had known they had taken the hamster and hidden it.

Then, when he was standing in the upstairs hall, outside of Maggie's room, he had heard a faint whirring sound. Only one thing could make that sound. A hamster in an exercise wheel.

He'd smiled, because he had all the clues to the puzzle. Vern and Michael had taken the hamster; and then while Pap and Junior had rushed out to the scene of the crime, they had come in the house, put Scooter—or whatever his name was—back in his cage, and carried him upstairs to Vern's room.

As Ralphie was standing in the hall, smiling, Maggie had slammed the door in his face, but the brilliance of his deductions would make her regret that.

Ralphie started up the steps for the second time that afternoon.

In the front yard, Vicki Blossom was saying, "What is

113

going on here? Can't I go away from home for five minutes without having a murder trial in my front yard?"

"Mom, Mud ate the school hamster and he's on trial for murder," Maggie explained.

"Has the world gone mad? Murder trials for horses. Now one for a hamster! I could just . . ."

Smiling, Ralphie entered Vern's room and picked up the cage. He went back down the stairs, opened the front door. His heart raced with pleasure.

He flung open the screen door and stood in the doorway, with the cage behind him. "The final piece of evidence," he said, "the final reason my client could not have committed murder is that there has been no murder!"

They were all looking at him. He loved it. He just loved it. Maybe he would be a real lawyer when he grew up. He sure had the brains for it. His brown eyes glinted like metal.

With that he brought out the cage. "Your honor, I give you—Scooty."

There was a moment of absolute and stunned silence, then total confusion. Vern and Michael were protesting that they hadn't had time to give their verdict and they had really worked on that verdict. They had practiced saying "Innocent" in unison until they had it down pat.

And, besides, they were the ones who had saved Scooty in the first place. It wasn't fair.

Junior, able to rise at last, got up from the witness stand. He went to the front door and dropped down on his knees in front of Scooty's cage.

Ralphie looked over Junior's head at Maggie. Her eyes were misty. Ralphie didn't like it when her eyes were filled with tears, but when her eyes were misty . . . well, it made him feel misty too.

Ralphie discovered that his favorite thing in the world was to be looked at with misty eyes.

Ralphie blinked.

These were not, as he had thought, the misty eyes of a person overcome by love and emotion. This mist was not an acknowledgment of his brilliance. This was not the mist that turned a man to mist too.

This mist chilled him to the bone, like a fog blown in from a wintry ocean. Ralphie shivered.

And then Maggie Blossom said words terrible enough to go with the mist, the worst words Ralphie had ever heard in his life.

"Ralphie?"

"Yes?"

"Ralphie, I hate you with all my heart!"

Junior was getting ready to beat up on Vern. His mom and Pap had given him permission. At first Junior had wanted to kill Vern and Michael, too, but Pap had stepped in.

"Now, now, you don't want to kill anybody."

"I do too!"

"You know what my daddy used to do when my brothers and I were boys?"

"No."

"I didn't tell you about that?"

"No."

"Well, if one brother was in the wrong, like Vern—Vern, you were in the wrong here. It was wrong to hide Scooty and make Junior think he was dead—well, when one of us was in the wrong, my daddy would take the heel of his shoe and he'd draw a big circle."

As he spoke, Pap moved around the yard, scratching a circle into the dirt with his heel.

"Then the brother who had done wrong would have to get in the circle."

Pap nodded to Vern, and Vern, shoulders sagging, stepped inside.

"Then what?"

"Then the other brother—that's you, Junior—the other brother would get in the circle, too, and start fighting. My daddy would time off three minutes on his pocket watch, like I'm getting ready to do.

"Vern, you can duck, you can dodge, you can run. You can do anything as long as you don't get out of the circle or hit Junior."

"Pap—"

"Them's the rules. Okay, Junior, you ready?"

Junior spit on his hands to show that he was.

"Vern?"

"I guess."

"Then go to it."

Junior paused before stepping over the line and into the circle. He said, "I'm doing this not only for myself, but for Mary as well."

"Mary?" Vern said.

"Yes, Mary," Junior answered.

Then, head as high as a knight's, he went forward into battle.

Chapter Twenty-one

The Trial after the Trial

MUD HAD BEEN READY TO COME OUT FROM UNDER THE house ever since he saw Dump in the jury box. Yet the memory of Junior's shouts and attempts at capture were still in his mind.

Finally, he got up from behind the apple crate and stretched. Keeping his body low, he moved to the steps. He paused at the truck tire and sat on his haunches.

The fight between Junior and Vern had just started, and Mud lay down by the tire to wait that out. His eyes turned to Dump, who was sitting beside Michael.

Michael was patting Dump, and Mud didn't like that. He also didn't like the fact that Dump was out there where Pap was, and he was under the house.

A fly landed on Mud's head, and he shook it off without taking his eyes from Dump.

The fight was in full swing now, but Mud continued to

watch Dump. Slowly, in a crouch, he began to inch forward.

"Pap, Vern won't let me hit him! He keeps jumping out of the way."

"That's what he's supposed to do, Junior."

"Well, I can't hit him if he won't stand still!"

"Keep trying. You've still got two minutes."

"There!"

"Pap, Junior hit me!"

"That's what he's supposed to do."

"Well, it left a mark on my arm. You didn't say he could leave marks."

"There!"

"Pap, that time he hit me when I was showing you where he hit me before! He's not playing fair."

"Well, you didn't play fair when you kidnapped Scooty. There!"

"Thirty-second warning," Pap called, eyeing his watch. "Twenty seconds . . . ten . . . three, two, one. All right, that's it. Shake hands."

Vern and Junior met in the center of the ring and reluctantly shook hands.

"Let's go in the house and see about supper."

Ralphie said, "Well, I guess I'd better be going if you guys are going to eat."

Maggie said, "That's the first good idea you've had all day."

She went in the house without looking back. Michael said, "Well, I guess I better be going." He left, and Vern and Junior went into the house. Pap and Dump followed.

Vicki and Pap stood on the steps, talking until the phone rang. Then they started up the steps. Vicki got to the front door first and Pap called, "That could be the police."

"It could be Rooney!" she called back.

Ralphie was left alone in the yard. He sighed.

Shoulders sagging, he went around the back of the house and picked up his bike. He could hear the Blossom family in the kitchen. The call was from a nurse at the hospital. "I'm going to see if they'll release her in my care," Pap said.

Vicki Blossom said, "That's all we need."

There didn't seem to be anything for Ralphie to do but go home. He threw one leg over his bike and pedaled off.

As he rounded the house, he saw Mud coming out from under the porch. Mud paused at the steps to move back and forth under the boards and let the porch scratch his back for him.

Then he went up the steps and barked at the screen door. Ralphie paused because it might be Maggie who would let Mud in. And Maggie might already be sorry she had been rude, and she might . . .

It was Maggie, but all she said was, "Come in, Mud." Mud went in the house with the rest of the Blossoms.

Ralphie went home.

Ralphie was sitting beside the telephone in his kitchen. Ralphie was taking deep breaths. Ralphie had heard of the medical condition called hyperventilation, and he thought he might be suffering from it.

Ralphie was getting ready to call Maggie.

It was now four hours since Mud's murder trial. Ralphie figured that four hours was about the length of time it would take for Maggie to get her senses back.

She could not possibly hate him. Not him . . . not her.

119

She could be mad enough to claim she hated him. She could be mad enough to think she hated him.

But it couldn't last. Maggie might even be sitting at her phone now, just as he was sitting at his, trying to get up the nerve to call and apologize.

Ralphie wasn't going to put her through that humiliation.

He would call and he would come out with one of those brilliant statements he was famous for—like the one about the Bible.

Ralphie wasn't sure what this particular brilliant statement would be, but he was confident that as soon as he heard her "hello," it would come. That was the good thing about having a brilliant mind—it came up with brilliance on its own.

Ralphie ran his hands through his curly hair, combing through the tangles. Then he wiped his hands on his jeans and reached for the phone.

Mud was in the kitchen trying to eat. He was having a hard time because Junior wouldn't leave him alone. Junior was hugging him and kissing him and talking to him.

Mud kept eating, but it wasn't easy.

"Mud, do you forgive me?" Junior was saying. "I'm sorry. I'm really and truly sorry."

Mud rolled his eyes in Junior's direction as he chewed. He didn't like to be fooled with while he was eating, but Junior would not be shaken off.

"Please forgive me, Mud." Junior raised the flap of Mud's ear so he could speak directly into the ear itself. "I'm sorry, Mud. Do you forgive me?"

"Naaw," Vern said from the table. He said it in a dog's voice.

Junior threw him a dirty look.

Mud shook his head to get his ear out of Junior's hand. The ear came free, but Junior still clung to his neck.

"Do you like me again?"

"Naw."

"Mom, make him stop! Because, Mud, I really, really like you. You're a good dog. Good, good dog." Junior smoothed Mud's long ears back from his face. "I didn't mean those things I said. You're a good dog. You wouldn't eat my Scooty, would you?"

"Yaaw," Vern growled.

"You better behave, Vern," Junior snapped. "Or Mom will let me beat you up again, won't you, Mom?"

"No, I don't like all this fighting." Vicki Blossom sighed. She wasn't eating in the hope that Rooney would still be able to take her out. "Why doesn't the phone ring? I—"

At that moment, as if on cue, the phone did ring.

"I'll get it," Vicki Blossom said. She jumped to her feet and crossed her fingers.

She turned her eyes to the ceiling. "I hope it's Rooney! Please, please let that horse trial be over. Please, please let it be Rooney. Please, please let me get in my new pants suit and have some fun!"

Ralphie was holding the phone so tightly his knuckles were turning white.

Aha! The phone was answered in the middle of the second ring.

Ralphie smiled tightly to himself.

Maggie had probably been sitting by the phone, praying for him to call. Then, just when she had given up and started in a dejected way for her room, the phone HAD rung!

121

It's Ralphie! her happy heart had cried, soaring like a kite. It's a miracle. Ralphie, oh, Ralphie! I'm coming!

"Hello!" There was such eagerness, such hope, in her hello that Ralphie's heart soared too. He had never before heard her voice like that.

Overcome by the girlish-womanliness of her "hello" and by his own eagerness to put her at her ease, to prove at once that he had not taken her cruel words seriously, he decided not to be brilliant but to be something he had rarely been in his lifetime—truthful.

"I love you," Ralphie said.

He was pleased with the way his voice sounded. Anytime a person said something he had never heard himself say before there was a certain risk that the words wouldn't sound right, but no movie star could have said "I love you" any better than . . .

Ralphie trailed off. There was a pause growing at the other end of the line.

For some reason, Ralphie thought of the radar-projected weather reports he saw occasionally on TV where a dangerous storm grew from a small white dot to a huge red pulsating storm system.

This pause was growing in the same uncontrollable, frightening way.

"Well, I'm glad somebody does," the voice on the phone snapped.

It was Mrs. Blossom's voice.

Ralphie felt the blood begin to drain from his head, leaving his brow in an icy sweat. Then the blood drained from his neck, his chest, from his body, leaving him as cold as an icicle.

He didn't know where the blood had gone, because his

whole entire body was cold, even his foot. Ralphie's shoulders began to shiver.

Ralphie let his lids close over his eyes.

He had told Mrs. Blossom that he loved her—Mrs. Blossom. M!R!S! Blossom. M**R**S B**L**O**—

But wait. Again, Ralphie stopped.

Maybe Mrs. Blossom hadn't recognized his voice. She didn't know how his "I love you's" sounded. She'd never heard one before. Nobody had. And it was going to be a long, long time, Ralphie thought, before anybody did again.

Ralphie opened his eyes. He was getting ready to very quickly, very quietly hang up the phone when he heard Mrs. Blossom put down her phone.

He didn't want to, but he kept listening. He listened while Mrs. Blossom moved away from the phone. He listened while she entered the kitchen. He listened while she began saying one terrible sentence after another.

"Maggie, it's for you. It's Ralphie. And guess what? He says he . . ."

Very quickly, very quietly, Ralphie hung up the telephone.

123

Chapter Twenty-two
The Fastest Man Alive

"RALPHIE."

The voice belonged to one of Ralphie's brothers.

Ralphie was in such misery he didn't know which brother it was. Anyway, Ralphie didn't care. They sounded alike, smelled alike, and Ralphie was not going to interrupt his misery by opening his eyes for the sight of a brother.

Besides, Ralphie was standing on his head so that his blood would run down into his brain and nourish it. Ralphie blamed his present condition on an undernourished brain. There was no other explanation for his telling Mrs. Blossom that—what he had told her.

"Ralphie."

"What?"

"Will you make Beanie a parachute?"

"No."

"Please."

"Who's Beanie?" Ralphie still did not open his eyes.

"Beanie is Frank's little brother and Beanie says if we make him a parachute, he'll jump off the roof."

"What roof?"

"The garage roof. He's already up there. And he says if we don't make him a parachute, he's going to jump off without one. We've got to get him a parachute. So will you?"

"No."

"Mom gave us a sheet."

"Does Mom know it's for a parachute?"

"No, she just asked if we were going to make anything dangerous."

"You don't call a parachute dangerous?"

"No! This parachute would save Beanie's life!"

Ralphie's brain was nourished enough so that he could imagine his mom's voice saying, "You made a parachute out of my king-size sheet? Well, I'm going to king-size you."

Ralphie still hadn't opened his eyes. Normally he would already have that parachute whipped out and attached to Beanie, but Ralphie wasn't normal. Indeed, Ralphie had never felt more subnormal in his life.

"Ralphie, telephone," his mother called.

At that, Ralphie opened his eyes.

This was the moment he had been dreading. It had now been two long days since he told Mrs Blossom he—since he told her what he told her—and he had known it was only a matter of time until Maggie called to taunt him.

"I'm not here," he called.

He knew the caller was Maggie. She was the only person who ever called him, and Ralphie could never speak to Maggie again.

125

His mother appeared in the doorway. "Ralphie! I said the telephone is for you."

"I'm not here."

"Get off your head and go to the phone."

"Mom, I'm letting blood go to my brain. My brain needs blood. It's not working right."

"Well, I don't deny your brain's not working, after you pushed your brothers down the hill in a Maytag box. But you boys have to learn right now that I'm not going to lie on the telephone for you."

Ralphie rolled his eyes to his brother. "Will you lie on the telephone for me?"

The brother said, "Sure, if you'll make the"—a sideways glance at his mother—"the you-know-what for Beanie."

"He is not lying for you or anybody else! Now, get off your head. It's Maggie on the phone, and she says there's an emergency."

"What kind of emergency?"

"She didn't say."

Ralphie got off his head and went to the phone. He felt as if he were going to his own hanging.

He wiped his hands before he picked up the phone. He swallowed. He said "Hello," then realized that in his nervousness he had not spoken aloud.

"Hello."

"Oh, Ralphie," Maggie said, "a terrible thing has happened."

At those words, Ralphie felt the first faint lessening of misery. He realized that while he had been balancing on his head with his eyes closed, suffering the greatest misery of his life, even then his luck had been working. The Ralphie luck. Something terrible actually had happened.

"What?"

127

"We finally found out what happened to Mad Mary."

"Oh?"

"She's in Alderson General Hospital."

Now Ralphie's mind clicked into high gear. His thoughts raced. Maggie was going to ask him to bust Mad Mary out of Alderson General Hospital. It was bound to be that. After all, he had once busted Junior out of the same hospital, and smuggled Mud in.

And he, Ralphie, was going to say yes.

Never mind that Mad Mary was probably hooked up to a machine. He'd unhook her. Never mind that she probably couldn't walk. He'd stolen wheelchairs before. Never mind that the hospital had probably burned all her clothes. He'd sew her some if he had to.

Maggie was saying, "I didn't want to call you because, you know, I was afraid you'd think I was, you know, using you again."

"No, no, it's all right. I want you to use me. Be my guest."

"Well, if you're sure . . ."

"I am!"

Ralphie couldn't stand the suspense. Also he was beginning to feel a sort of enthusiasm for the caper.

"You want me to bust Mad Mary out of the hospital, right? And if that's what you want, that's what you'll get. I'll bust her out of Alderson so fast the nurses won't know she's gone—"

"No, no!" Maggie laughed. "No, she's getting out on her own. Well, Pap's getting her out. But she wants her cane— you know that long crook she walks with?"

"I remember," Ralphie said.

Indeed, he could recall the exact feel of that cane. Mad Mary had loaned it to him and Maggie the night they climbed the tree after the Green Phantom. It was the night he had kissed Maggie. He wasn't likely to forget anything about that night.

"Well, see, what happened, Ralphie, was that Mad Mary passed out beside the road—right where we found her bag. Guess what she passed out from?"

"I couldn't." Ralphie's blood was still racing from thoughts of hospital escapades and treetop embraces.

"Malnutrition and worms."

"Well, that figures."

"I knew it couldn't be good for her to eat stuff off the road! It's not nourishing! The doctor says from now on she has to buy her meat at Bi-Lo."

"Smart man."

"Anyway, some people were driving by and saw her. She had passed out in the ditch. So they loaded her in their car and took her to Alderson General. Only they left her bag and her cane."

"Well, leaving that bag made sense."

"We've got the bag—it's hanging on our kitchen door-knob, and I told Pap I'd go back for the cane; but, Ralphie, I'm not sure I remember the exact spot. Do you?"

The exact spot where he had entwined a flower into Maggie's braid. You bet he remembered . . .

And then Ralphie sat up straight in his chair. He smiled for the first time since he had told Mrs. Blossom—what he had told her. His smile widened to a grin. Ralphie beamed.

For Ralphie remembered the last time he had seen Mad Mary's cane. It had been in the Blossom kitchen. That cane was in the Blossom kitchen! It was leaning against the back door beside the bag! But if Maggie wanted to pretend the cane was still lost in the weeds in order to see

129

him . . . well, he would pretend the cane was still lost in the weeds.

Ralphie said in a mature voice, "I remember."

"Oh, Ralphie, then will you meet me there?"

Ralphie took a deep breath, and he said the words he had wanted to say, yearned to be man enough to say, ever since he met Maggie.

"It's a date."

Ralphie hung up the phone. If he hurried . . .

Ralphie knew that speed was not something a person with an artificial leg was usually good at. He was different. He prided himself on his lightning fast reactions. Once in English class the teacher had asked the members of the class to write something about themselves. Ralphie had written:

I am the fastest man on earth. I drive my bike up mountains without slowing down. I have been known to run to New York City and back during recess. I hold the world record for the Indy 500. To let off steam one Saturday afternoon, I dug a hole to China, had tea, and filled the hole back up in time for the family barbecue. When I am bored, I race eighteen-wheelers on the freeway.

At this moment, he felt it was not an exaggeration. In moments like this, he was the fastest man alive.

Not only would he break the world record getting to Maggie, but he would also whip out Beanie's parachute before he left.

After all, a child's life was at stake.

Chapter Twenty-three
By Hook or by Crook

MAGGIE WAS RIDING SANDY BOY THROUGH THE WOODS, taking a shortcut to the place where she and Ralphie had found Mad Mary's bag. At her side, like a knight's lance, was Mad Mary's crook.

Maggie rode in an easy, unhurried way, but her thoughts were not on the woods or the horse or the golden afternoon. Maggie's thoughts were on Ralphie.

When Maggie first learned that Ralphie had told her mother he loved her, she had felt her hatred solidify.

She had heard the news at the supper table along with all the other Blossoms. "It's Ralphie," her mom had said, returning from the phone. "He says he loves me, but hopefully he thought I was you. I'm not that desperate—yet."

"Is he still on the phone?" Maggie had asked.

"Yes."

Maggie pushed her chair back and stood up. She flung her braids behind her back, out of the way.

"Well, he's got his nerve calling after I told him I hated him with all my heart."

"Maggie, honey, make it short, please. Rooney could still call."

"It'll be short, all right."

Maggie had gotten up, walked quickly to the phone, and picked it up. She was ready for the conversation.

He would say, "Maggie?" in an uncertain way. It would be satisfying to hear Ralphie being uncertain, but that would just be the beginning.

She would say, "Yes, this is Maggie, the daughter of the woman you love."

He would fall silent. She had never heard him silent before, but that would not weaken her hatred any more than his uncertainty would.

She picked up the phone, but she didn't get to say anything. The dial tone buzzed in her ear. Ralphie was gone.

Maggie let the telephone rest on her shoulder for a moment. There was a finality about that dial tone, as if it wasn't just the end of a telephone call. That dial tone meant that Ralphie was not going to call again—ever. Ralphie was not going to come see her again—ever. Ralphie was out of her life.

From her shoulder, came the operator's voice, "If you'd like to make a call, please hang up and . . ."

Maggie hung up and went back to the kitchen.

"So what did Ralphie say?" Junior asked with interest.

"Nothing."

"Does he love you or Mom?"

Maggie shrugged. "Who cares?"

132

Maggie wasn't good at arranging meetings with boys and that is why it took her until Sunday to think up a way to see Ralphie. She would have to ask his help.

Maggie had done this before—he had helped her sneak Mud into Alderson General Hospital to see Pap, she had asked him to help find Junior when he was lost. He had even come up with helium when the Green Phantom was in trouble.

Finally, she came up with it. She would ask Ralphie's help in finding Mad Mary's cane. Of course, she had already found it. She and Pap and Junior had gone back that same evening, and there it was. But Ralphie didn't know that.

Now she was heading toward the spot to meet Ralphie, and she was on horseback. She wanted to get there fast, hide the cane, and be standing there when Ralphie arrived.

She came through the trees and reined Sandy Boy to a stop. This was the spot. Maggie slid off Sandy Boy's back. She looked around. The bag had been right about here. She paced it off. So the crook should be right about here.

Maggie dropped the crook in the tall grass. She brushed the grass over it. She wasn't satisfied. It was too obvious. She took the crook and dropped it closer to the trees so that it was camouflaged by the fallen branches and twigs.

Then she walked to the ditch and sat down.

Holding Sandy Boy's reins in one hand, she watched the road for Ralphie's bike.

Ralphie was in battle dress.

He had on black jeans, black T-shirt—both faded to a

133

gun-metal gray—and black, high-top sneakers, untied, with the laces whipping around his ankles.

Ralphie was bent over the handlebars of his bike, head down, eyes squinting into the wind.

With every spin of the wheels, his heart sang.

Ralphie to the rescue! Ralphie, the fastest man alive, is on the way!

He came over the crest of the hill, and he saw Maggie at once. She was sitting beside the road, holding Sandy Boy's reins.

When she saw him, she got up and brushed off the seat of her jeans.

Ralphie rested back on the seat of his bicycle and coasted down the hill. He was letting his natural brilliance coast downhill in the same way. He was not—no matter what restraint it took—he was not going to be brilliant.

After all, it took real brilliance to find just the right tone of non-brilliance.

Ralphie braked right in front of Maggie, stopping on a dime, as the saying went. He laid his bike on its side, and the rear wheel continued to spin as he turned to Maggie.

"Now," he said, with studied non-brilliance, "let me be of assistance."

"Where have you been with Mary's cane? I was looking for that," Junior said when Maggie and Ralphie rode up.

Maggie was on Sandy Boy, Ralphie on his bike. "Here," Maggie said quickly. She handed down the crook.

"Thanks, I wanted to be the one to give it to her."

Junior sat back down on the steps with the crook across his knees. His eyes watched the bridge for the sight of Pap's truck. He had been sitting on the steps, waiting, ever since Pap had left for town.

134

Maggie said, "Want to come to the barn with me, Ralphie?"

"I guess."

Beside Junior on the steps was Scooty's cage. Ever since the miraculous moment when he had learned Scooty was alive, Junior had not let Scooty out of his presence. Scooty had even slept beside Junior in his bed.

Junior saw the truck turn off the highway. He got quickly to his feet and ran down the steps, forgetting Scooty in his excitement. Then he ran back, got Scooty, and ran across the yard.

By this time the truck had come to a stop. Junior was jiggling with excitement. He was going to see his best friend in the world and he had so much to tell her—about Scooty, about the trial, about . . . oh, everything. He wouldn't be able to shut up for a hundred years—that's how much he had to tell her.

Mary got out of the truck and Junior's words died. His excitement did too.

This wasn't Mary. This wasn't his friend. This woman was clean. He would never have recognized her in a million years. This could have been just any woman in the grocery store or in the drugstore.

And Pap had said, "I'm going to try to get Mary to stay the night."

And Junior had said, when he still thought she was the woman he knew and loved, "She can sleep in my room with me and Scooty!"

Pap had tried to warn him. "She's bound to look different from what we're used to, Junior. A stay in the hospital don't help a person."

"I know! I went in the hospital one time and came out with two broken legs!"

"Well, if you're sure."

"Oh, I'm sure. Like, I spent the night with her in her cave and now she'll spend the night with me in my room, and then I'll spend the night in her cave and she'll . . ."

Spending the night with his friend Mary was one thing, but spending the night with a grocery-store stranger was another.

Behind Junior, Mud pushed open the screen door. He stood for a moment while the door banged shut behind him.

Junior turned. "No barking, Mud, I mean it. I was supposed to put you in the basement. Now, watch Dump and see how nicely he behaves. You could learn a lot from Dump."

Mud came down the steps and Junior twisted his fingers in Mud's bandana. Mud twisted free and ran the rest of the way to the truck.

Mary threw up her thin arms for protection, but Mud was just hurrying to greet Pap. Even Mud didn't recognize a clean Mad Mary.

Junior pulled himself toward the truck. His feet felt heavier than usual, so his walking was slow. His shoes left long reluctant marks in the dirt.

Junior had never expected to see anything like Mad Mary in his life. It was as if she had been disguised by experts.

Her clothes were new. Her hair had been washed. They'd even combed it!

"Well, Junior!" she said. Junior was grateful that her voice was the same.

"Your cane."

Junior presented it in a formal way, with a little bow, and then he stepped back out of the way.

She took the cane and held it against her as if it were something that had been lost for years, not just days. "Oh, Junior, maybe my life's going to get back together after all."

"Mine did."

She took a few steps with her cane as if to make sure it was really hers.

"Your bag's in the kitchen."

"You and I seem to go through the same things, don't we, Junior?" she said as they started toward the house. "Because you know what I thought of in the hospital?"

"What?"

"I thought of you waking up in the same hospital and not knowing where you were. That's just what happened to me."

"And it was scary, wasn't it?"

"Yes, it was."

"See, I told you." Junior glanced over at Pap. "Pap, I told her that waking up and not knowing where you were was the scariest thing that can happen to a person, but she didn't believe me."

"Well, I believe you now."

"You're going to sleep in my room," Junior said firmly. "You can have the bed and Scooty and I will sleep on the floor."

"I wouldn't want to put you and Scooty out."

Junior was warming to Mary. She didn't look the same. She didn't smell the same. But the important thing—she was the same.

"You won't put us out. We're very, very glad to have you."

Chapter Twenty-four

The Changing of Ralphie's Eyes

EVER SINCE RALPHIE HAD TOLD MRS. BLOSSOM THAT HE —what he had told her—Ralphie had been dreading the moment when he would see her again.

In his worst nightmares, Mrs. Blossom had smiled in an amused way and said something like, "Well, if it isn't my admirer."

In his one good nightmare, she had given him an amused, knowing smile —but not so Maggie could see it— and kept her thoughts to herself.

Ralphie and Maggie were in the barn when the dreaded meeting took place. Maggie was unsaddling Sandy Boy, and Ralphie was standing back, concentrating on not being brilliant, when Mrs. Blossom walked into the barn.

Ralphie stepped back with alarm. His face began to burn.

"Don't bother unsaddling him," Vicki Blossom said. "I'm going for a ride myself."

Ralphie pressed back into the bales of hay. He looked down at the floor, faking interest in the dirt, the manure, the straw-strewn boards. He figured if he didn't actually see the amused smile, he could pretend it hadn't been there.

"I thought you were waiting for Rooney's call," Maggie said.

"I got the call. He can't come till next weekend."

Vicki Blossom got into a saddle as easily as ordinary people get into dining room chairs.

"Which might as well be next year for all the good it does me."

"He'll come, Mom."

"Sure, he'll come. IF there are no more horse trials. I always did detest people who were cruel to horses, and now I have an extra reason to detest them."

Sandy Boy neighed with pleasure and tossed his head as she took the reins. He never did that for anybody but Vicki Blossom. He allowed Maggie to ride him—he wouldn't even buck when Vern or Junior got on—but Sandy Boy was Vicki's horse in the way Mud was Pap's dog.

"Plus, if he doesn't come soon, my pants suit is going to look funny. It's got short sleeves. I'll have to wear a coat over it! And where am I going to get the money for a good-looking coat?"

She touched her heels to Sandy Boy's sides, and they were off.

As the sound of Sandy Boy's hooves faded into the distance, the breath went out of Ralphie in one long sigh of relief.

What a nice family this was, he thought. What a nice

140

world. What a nice woman Vicki Blossom had turned out to be.

Ralphie stopped in surprise. Two days ago he had told Vicki Blossom he loved her by mistake. Today, he could have told her the same thing and almost meant it.

Junior was in the kitchen, seated across the table from Mad Mary. Scooty was in his cage on the table between them.

Junior was leaning forward with his chin resting on his hands. He and Mary had been in the kitchen together for an hour. And gradually Mary was beginning to turn into her old self. Junior had already stopped missing her old smell of smoke, grease, and sweat, and gotten used to soap.

Junior said, "I really thought you were dead, I really and honestly thought that."

"Why, Junior, I'm sorry I caused you to worry," Mad Mary said.

"Not you, Mary. I was talking to Scooty."

"Oh." A smile cracked Mary's old face.

"I knew you weren't dead."

"Well, *I* sure didn't," Mary said. "How did you know that?"

"It's simple." Junior shrugged. "You're my best friend in the world. If something had happened to you, I would have known it."

"Ah," said Mary.

"Ralphie," Maggie said, "you're going to think this is just my imagination."

"Probably," Ralphie admitted, "but go ahead and try me."

"Well, it's just that, you know, I can always tell when you want to kiss me."

Since Ralphie pretty much wanted to kiss her all the time, this didn't seem too surprising. He decided not to comment.

"Don't you want to know how I can tell?" Maggie asked, glancing at him sideways.

"I guess."

"Your eyes change color."

Ralphie straightened his shoulders in a quick defensive movement.

"They do not."

"Yes, they do."

"They do not. I would know if my eyes changed color."

"It's true," she went on firmly. "Normally your eyes are light brown, but when you want to kiss me, Ralphie, they turn dark and murky."

"They do not. You're making that up. My eyes have never been dark and murky in their lives. I resent that description."

"Dark and murky," Maggie repeated. "I'm not making it up. I'm only describing it."

"Well, I don't believe it."

"Next time you come over, I'm going to pull out a pocket mirror and prove it."

"So what color are my eyes now?"

Maggie checked.

"Hmmm, dark and murky."

"See, that proves you're lying because the last thing in this world I want to do right now is kiss you. I'm going to take my eyes and go home."

"So, go."

"I mean it," he said, though he made no attempt to

leave. "Why would I want to kiss a girl who goes around insulting my eyes?" He came closer. "So what color are they now?"

Maggie looked. "Actually, a little bit murkier."

"Huh." Ralphie didn't care what color his eyes were as long as Maggie kept looking in them. They could be purple with orange dots for all he cared.

Anyway, he hadn't known a person's eyes could change color. He wished he'd had this bit of information sooner. He could have been watching to see if her eyes changed.

He looked into Maggie's eyes.

He would have given anything to see red and white pinwheels spinning around. But Maggie's eyes were the same clear green they always were. Here he was with eyes so murky he could hardly see out of them and here she was with eyes as clear as jewels.

Maggie grinned. "Thanks for helping me find the cane."

"I was glad to."

"And Ralphie?"

"What?"

"You know, sometimes you do seem almost human."

"Sometimes I am."

Ralphie's thoughts were racing. Maybe green eyes didn't change. Why should they? Green was the international color for GO, wasn't it? And GO was exactly what Ralphie wanted to do.

Ralphie lowered his head. He felt encouraged by the fact that Maggie's head was still tilted up.

He kissed her.

Once.

Her face was still turned up and he felt he could kiss her again.

Twice, maybe three times.

But Ralphie decided to play it cool.

He said, "Now, don't expect me to do that every time my eyes get murky, Maggie. Half the time my eyes get murky just because they feel like getting murky."

Maggie's grin broadened so that he could see her pointed tooth. "I'll try not to."

Ralphie grinned back at her. "I just didn't want you to get your hopes up and be disappointed."

In the silence that followed, there was muffled laughter from the bushes, and then a chorus of, "Maggie and Ralphie up in a tree, k-i-s-s-i-n-g . . ."

Ralphie swirled around, his hands on his slim hips. "Come on, you guys, cut it out. This is a tree? Use your heads. Look, you want us to kiss in a tree? Come on, Maggie, let's find a tree and climb up it and kiss so your little brother and his infantile friend can hop around yelling—"

But Maggie was laughing too hard to answer.

Chapter Twenty-five

The New Invention

Junior had not been as sorry to see Monday come as he had thought. Pap had been right about Scooty. The whole thing was to teach responsibility, and Junior did not want any more lessons in that.

He would be glad to—well, he would be willing to—take lessons in reading and writing and spelling, even arithmetic. But he did not want any more lessons in responsibility. As far as Junior was concerned, he had earned an A in responsibility.

The school bus pulled up, the door opened, and Vern and Junior and Scooty got on. The first seat was vacant, and Junior took it. Vern went to the back of the bus to sit by Michael.

Junior sat with the cage on his lap as he had on Friday, but—unlike Friday—Junior was not talking to Scooty in low, excited whispers. Nor was he jiggling his legs.

The bus made another stop. The Rankin girls got on and moved to the back of the bus.

Junior thought with sympathy of the person who would be selected to take Scooty home next weekend, a person who would be full of excitement and the desire to provide pleasure for his houseguest, only to find out about the most terrible thing in the entire world—responsibility.

It was funny, Junior thought. He had looked forward to the weekend and looked forward to the weekend, and it had been terrible. It had turned out all right—as things usually did with the Blossoms—but while it was going on, it had just been terrible.

Rebecca, from Junior's room at school, got on the bus. "Hi, Junior."

"Hi."

She stuck her finger through the cage and wiggled it. "How're you doing, Scooty?"

"Say 'Fine.' " Junior had always admired the way mothers answered for their babies like this.

"Did you have fun at Junior's, Scooty?"

"Say 'Part of the time.' "

"Mind if I sit with you?"

"Me?"

She nodded.

Junior was relieved to be answering for himself. "No, I wouldn't mind."

She sat down.

This was the first time a girl—no, anybody!—this was the first time anybody had wanted to sit by Junior on the school bus, so he felt complimented. Perhaps she only wanted to sit by Scooty, but he hoped not.

Rebecca stuck her finger back through the wires to

wiggle hello again to Scooty. "I hope I get to take him home this weekend."

"Oh, no," Junior said in alarm. Just a moment ago he had been feeling sympathy for someone, and what if it turned out to be Rebecca—the only person in the entire school who had ever wanted to sit by him on the bus?

"Why do you say that? Oh, no?"

"Rebecca, a hamster is a lot of responsibility."

"I think it would be fun."

Junior paused. He didn't want to spoil anybody's fun, especially not Rebecca's, but he was wise beyond his years in responsibility and hamsters.

"Will you let me give you one bit of advice?"

"What's that?"

"Whatever you do, don't make him a tunnel."

In the back of the bus Michael and Vern were going over the events of the past two days. Michael started the conversation.

"I can't believe everything turned out all right."

"I can't either."

"I can't believe we got our backpacks."

"Me either."

"Did Mad Mary say anything to you?"

"About what?"

"Us trespassing in her cave."

"No."

"Do you think she recognized you?"

"Yes."

"I can't believe everything turned out all right."

"Remember Scooty?"

"And the trial?"

"And k-i-s-s-i-n-g."

147

And their laughter was loud enough to make the Rankin girls turn around.

"What's funny?" they asked.

Junior hurried up the stairs to the school, down the hall, and into his classroom.

"Junior, why you're early," the teacher said. "You're the first one here. You almost beat me."

"I wanted to return Scooty."

"Did you enjoy him?"

"A little bit of the time," Junior said truthfully.

Junior put the cage on the hamster table and took his seat. He was glad to have a little time to himself. Because on the bus that morning Junior had had an idea.

He didn't dare to hope that it would turn into an invention, and besides Rebecca kept talking to him. Rebecca was a good talker—her specialty was TV shows she'd seen—and listening to her tell about shows was better than watching them. Junior didn't have time to think.

Now he did have a few private moments, and a thrill of creativity came over Junior. He closed his eyes.

He was going to make something. And unlike the wings, the coyote trap, the UFO, and the tunnel of doom, this invention was going to work.

What a good weekend this one was going to be. The horse detective was going to come, and the horse detective could see what Junior was going to make! The more people there were to admire his inventions, the better Junior liked it.

Junior opened his eyes. Junior smiled.